The Journals
Washington State

By Marilyn Carlsson

PRINTED IN THE UNITED STATES OF AMERICA

Cover art by Nancy Calkins
ISBN: 979-8-9884715-1-6

For my family and friends who wanted more.

It has been about a year or so since I was able to rescue my sister and her friend Jim from a portal/vortex thing in Alaska.

I had promised Mike and his parents that if I found my sister and Jim, we would all get together. Getting back to Anchorage was not difficult but we did keep it very low key. We did not want any crazy attention if our story got out. I think all the others felt the same way as during our time in Anchorage, we did not see anything in the newspapers or on news reports. We were there for about a week before we all got together. We had a lot to do. Marni and Jim needed clothes, shoes, basically everything. Marni had some stuff that the police gave me, but Jim had nothing. Mike, his parents, Parker, and our guides along with Harold and his brother Mark got together. We have not heard from Allen, the fourth person that came out of the vortex with us. He did not attend and none of us have heard from him since getting to Anchorage. I hope he is doing well. We all promised to stay in touch, but you know how that goes sometimes, life gets in the way. Harold said to give him a call if I ever need a guide again.

My sister, Marni and Jim do not talk about what happened or what they went through while missing and I don't talk about it either. They are, I am happy to say, doing well and getting back to their normal lives. Jim, thanks to his ex-wife and son had a business to go back to. My sister was a different story. Her employer would not take her back and she lost all her belongings and her apartment. But I am happy to say she found a much better job that she is happy with and is thinking of finding a small condo or townhome to buy. We now stay in touch and get together when we can.

One thing that I have kept doing from my Alaskan trip is keeping a journal. Nothing earth shattering, just everyday things, accept one thing……

There is one thing that I have not told anyone. Something happened to me when I was in the vortex to rescue my sister. I see and feel things that I did not before. I think they are spirits/ghosts, but I'm not sure. I have not tried to interact with what I'm seeing as it sort of freaks me out. I just pretend that they are not there. I try not to look at them because I don't want them to know I can see them. So far it has worked. It's very disorienting and scary sometimes. I think that is the reason I have not done much this past year. I have been trying to figure this thing out, to see if there is any way to control it and I may have. Only time will tell, and I still have to get brave enough to try and talk to the people I see. I do have to say it has been a very interesting year. I wonder what Parker will say, if I decide to tell him.

Parker and I have stayed in touch over the past year or so after our Alaska adventure. Somehow over time I just started calling him Parker rather than Ben. I think I just like Parker better and he has not corrected me. As a thank you for his help in finding my sister I have invited him on a trip. I still need pin him down as to where he wants to go. I will be giving him a call in the next day or two. I have a lot of questions for him. First, where would he like to go? A big city like New York, Chicago, LA, the list can go on. Is he interested in anything unusual? He may be after our adventure in Alaska. Who would have thought that vortexes are real. I'm still not sure where I was when I was in there or how much time went by. Maybe he would like ghost hunting? That would be right up my ally, especially now that I see things. We will see.

WASHINGTON STATE

April 17

Ok, I talked to Parker, and he surprised me. Really. He wants to go to the Pacific Northwest, Washington State to be exact. Why? He wants to see if we can find Bigfoot! Really! I asked what brought this on. He said that he had always been intrigued by the multiple reported sightings, not really believing but after what we experienced, he is curious and would like to try to see if it is real. He wanted to know if this would be too much for me or would I be up to it. I told him that I'm game!

I asked Parker why not search for Bigfoot in Alaska? He thought that Alaska was just too big. He mentioned that there was one place in Alaska, Portlock, a ghost town for years, that would be a great place to check out, but it was very remote, and that Bigfoot had driven the people from the village years ago. He said that it was also hard to get there and if something happened, it was hard to get help. I told him that he would need to tell me about it when we get together, that he had peeked my interest.

He believed that the Pacific NW would be a better choice. He said that he had done some research and had an area in mind. He said believe it or not there is an area close to Carson in Washington State, a National Forest called Gifford Pinchot. I looked up Gifford and it is fascinating. According to what I could find it has basically been inhabited forever. The forest service is still identifying archaeological sites. Maybe a side trip to check out the sites when we're not looking for Bigfoot. It's also close to a place called Ape Canon. He said that we could try there too if we have time but thought Gifford would be a better choice. I said ok, that I would do some research on the area and let him know my thoughts. I asked how long of a trip he would be willing to do. He said two maybe three weeks, leaving and if possible, at the end of this month. If that would not be too soon. He stopped and got serious and said, "Sara you do not have to do this". I told him that yes, I did and wanted to, and that I would be emailing him some questions regarding the trip and to get back to me as soon as he can as we do not have a lot of time to plan this out. Well, the email is sent. Some of the questions I asked were what type of accommodations would suit him, rustic or not. I did mention that I thought two cars would be best so if one of us needed to get something from a store the other would not be stranded. Also, any food and drink preferences. I'll see what he come up with.

April 22

It has been a very busy five days. Everything is arranged. We will both be flying out on April 30th and meeting at the Portland International Airport. I have arranged two cars. Parker agreed with me regarding two cars, so neither of us will be stranded if one of us is using the car. We will be staying in a house that I rented about thirty-eight miles from the airport. Parker had no preference regarding where we stayed. The house I found is close to Gifford Pinchot and some towns for supplies. The home is on the edge of a National Forest and in the vicinity of Ape Canyon. It has a gourmet kitchen, three bedrooms, and two and a half baths. The pictures really look nice, I hope it is. There is a general store close by and other stores a little way out. I plan on arranging other items that I think we will need on the internet.

Well, that's all for now, there is more planning to do on the net for all the stuff we will need to rent or buy, and I need to do more research on Bigfoot in the area. What is the history? Why there?

April 27

Looking into Bigfoot has been as interesting as the missing people in Alaska. Bigfoot has been around for a very long time and seems to be on every continent. The Indigenous people of the area and other areas in the country have their own names. Some I have not added here as they are in the language of the "people" but some that I am familiar with are Grassman, Sasquatch, Yeti and Yowie.

Some of the Indigenous people think of Bigfoot as a messenger. Warning the people of danger. Others believe that Bigfoot exists in another dimension and can appear in our dimension wherever they need to or choose to, that there is always a reason. That he is from God and like a big brother that looks out for them.

I can go on and on about what the people think. It comes down to that he is a messenger with a warning that the people are not taking care of the land or themselves.

It is also said Bigfoot has psychic abilities, that he knows when people are searching for him, and that he can choose who he will appear to and help him evade capture.

Well learning that, this may be a lost cause before we even try. Parker being a cop may have and I'm sure has done his own research. Once we get there and are settled, we can compare notes.

April 28

Received confirmation from my favorite travel agent, Amy, and we leave on the 30th. She has arranged the flights and the cars. I took care of renting the house as I was afraid someone else would book it. She has emailed Parker the info he needs so we are all set.

Now the hard part……I need to pack.

April 29

I spent the day making arrangements for my mail to be held. Went to the bank for some cash. Cleaned out the fridge, so no bad food or smells when I get home.

One thing that I discovered is that I really need to start working on my packing skills. I must have packed and unpacked four or five times yesterday trying to decide what to bring. Even with the packing issue, I am packed and ready to go.

April 30

Ok, I have walked through my house, double checked everything, and set the alarm. I am good to go. The cab ride should not be too long, and I have given myself a few hours in order to get there well before my flight. Parker's flight will be shorter than mine, but Amy has set the flights so that we will arrive within an hour or so of each other. Have to go, my cab is here.

Parker was already there and had looked up my flight info and met me at the gate. It was so great to see him in person again after all this time. He actually looked the same as last year. We made our way to the car rental and off we went. The ride to the house was not bad but the sun was setting as we arrived. We did not take time to look around on the ride. We hauled our stuff in and explored the house a little. We picked our rooms, me getting the bigger of the two master suites and moved our luggage into them. I knew we would be getting in a little late, so I asked the owner to stock some items in the frig, sandwich stuff with chips, along with beer and other liquid libations. We had a little something to eat and a drink or two and went our separate ways. Tomorrow was going to be busy.

May 1

I was up early. After wandering through the house and checking out all the rooms, Parker found me out on the deck with a cup of coffee just staring at the view. It was amazing. Trees, the forest as far as the eye could see and then you had the mountains in the distance. He had his own cup of coffee and just sat down without a word, and we just sat there looking and taking it all in. Don't get me wrong, Alaska was amazing, but I did not see it this way, looking over a small valley with everything stretched out into the National Park. I think I was too focused on finding Marni to really appreciate Alaska.

After a while we went our separate ways to get cleaned up so we could get our day started and it would be a busy one. I had a list and I'm sure Parker had one too.

Over breakfast and more coffee, we went over our lists. I told him that I had arranged for stuff at the general store and that anything that I forgot, or he thought we needed we could get there or order it. We agreed that as much as we wanted to hit the forest trails, some almost just outside our back door, we needed to prepare. We were so excited to get going but we agreed to wait a couple of days to do that.

We took one car to the store, and we probably should have taken both. I did not realize how much stuff I purchased or rented. At least we have a couple of days to go through everything and if we don't need it we can send/bring it back.

I think Parker was impressed with what items I had arranged for as many of the items were on his list too. We basically went through everything, organizing and putting together if necessary. We decided about three in the afternoon that we were done for the day and that we would concentrate on a drink or two while catching up, enjoy the view, dinner and then lights out.

It was great catching up. I think this is really the first time we talked about our lives. I found out that Parker is single, and currently not dating. He does not think being a cop and having a wife and family would work out well as some of his co-workers have troubled marriages. He said it was the stress of the job and some cannot get over the authority thing at home. He hoped to one day find someone after he leaves the force. I did not tell him much about myself and kept steering the conversation to work and hobbies. It was a great end to our day. We turned in early as tomorrow will be a busy day of going through all items we have and prioritizing them and going for groceries.

May 2

This morning was much the same as yesterday. We cannot get over the view. Sitting there Parker got a serious look on his face. He asked if I wanted more coffee. I said yes and asked what was wrong. He got the coffee and sat down. He said that it was most likely none of his business, and I could tell him that it was not, and it would be done. Ok what was this about? He took a deep breath and said that this had been bothering him and he just came out and asked how can you afford to do all this? The plane, first class? Two cars, the house, equipment……? He was feeling like he was taking advantage, not pulling his weight and worried that I could not afford all this and that I was just going into debt to repay him for Alaska, basically doing what a cop does…find people. He also added that any payment was not expected for helping me find Marni and if I were going into debt, he wanted me to cancel the rest of the trip and we would head home.

I liked him before and now I really like him, bless his honesty and caring, but I was afraid to tell him the truth. I just sat there stunned. Most people would not care about me and would just look for a way to drain me dry if they knew. Thinking that, I decided to tell him the truth.

I told him that before I went to look for my sister, we were estranged from each other, and I had not seen her for a number of years. Why was no longer important. I told him that during that time I had played the Lotto and won and that even my sister did not know. That I won really, big, and just waited for his reaction. He looked at me and laughed and said really, no, tell me the truth. He wanted to know if I was paying for all this with a home equity loan or some other loan, a refi of my house. He knows my address and that I do not live extravagantly with a large house, but in a very nice area or that I have expensive stuff. I am still just me.

Bless this man. Without telling him how much I won, how will I convince him that this trip was not draining my finances. I just sat there and waited. He kept looking at me waiting for me to confess to a home equity or refi loan. When that did not happen, he stopped and looked at me and said are you serious? I just smiled, patted his hand, said yes and do you want more coffee?

It was great. He had no idea what to say but said yes, that I assumed was for more coffee. I knew that this conversation was not over, just on hold while he processed this information. I also had some thinking to do as to how I would handle the subject when it came up again and I knew it would.

After a little while I mentioned that we needed to get to the grocery store and get the stuff he wanted and what I wanted or missed on my list from other stores. I suggested that we separate, divide, and conquer. He was ok with that, and I asked if he wanted my credit card. Big mistake. I think that I insulted him. I did not mean to. He said NO and left with a list. Oboy, this was not good. This is not what I wanted. I was not trying to make him feel small, inadequate or hell I don't know. I'll have to think about this while getting stuff on my list. The errands will give us both time to think. This afternoon and evening I am not looking forward to.

Will the trip be over before it really begins? I guess I'll find out later.

I got back before Parker; I was hoping to. I got everything put away when I heard the car pull in. I had no idea what to expect. Would he still be really pissed off, pack and leave? He came in with his arms full of bags and I went to help. Good sign, he accepted my help and said there was more in the car. After we got everything in and put away, in silence, I asked if I could make us a drink, sit out on the deck and talk. He agreed.

We both started talking at once. He said you go first. I told him that I did not mean to hurt or belittle him asking if he wanted my credit card. It was just that I did not want him to have any expenses on this trip as it was my gift to him. Then I waited. He just sat there looking out into the forest and I believe trying to figure out how to tell me that he would be leaving.

I was surprised when he said that he may have overreacted. He felt like it was a slap in the face that he could not contribute to the trip. He said that he understands that I won a lot of money, but he could buy things that we need too. I apologized and said that I would not ask him about my credit card again. He looked at me and said that he would ask for it if something was really, really expensive. He grinned and we both laughed and then I asked, so what's for dinner.

Over dinner I asked him about Portlock. He said that the history of it is fascinating. The area had been inhabited by the Aleuts for centuries and is located on the edge of the Kenai Peninsula. The area was named after Captain Nathaniel Portlock, a British sea captain who sailed there in 1786. The village was established and in 1921 a Post Office was opened. The town was an active cannery in the early-twentieth century. In the 1940's it was reported that hunters had disappeared in the hills outside of town. People have been disappearing for years, equipment being destroyed but the final blow to the village was when dismembered bodies of some of the missing washed up in the lagoon. The villagers abandoned the site for fear of their lives and blamed it on Bigfoot, locally known as Nantinaq.

We talked for a while after dinner and finally decided to call it a night. It was later than I thought when I got back to my room, but I had to write this down…. fascinating. Maybe someday……...

May 3

I thought I was an early riser. Parker was up, dressed and had coffee made with stuff out for breakfast. We both prepared breakfast and while eating talked about our day. We agreed to go through our lists, pull things together and get ready to start our search the next day.

We worked most of the day inventorying what we had and packing our backpacks. We must have packed and then unpacked them multiple times in order to bring less stuff, only what we thought we would really need. One thing we did talk about was we would need to pack differently for overnight outings. Parker came up with a great idea. He said why don't we separate the items, overnight items that we think we need into one section of the garage and day trip items on the other side. What a great idea as the cars were not being parked in the garage. We also agreed that for the first few days we would only do day trips to get our bearings and to scout out an area for a longer search. One thing that we realized as we were doing this was that we did not have any local maps or a map of the National Park or the area. Yes we had our phones but a real map would show so much more of the area. Parker said he would run into town and see what they had and get what he thought we might need. I had this overpowering urge to ask if he wanted my credit card as a joke but resisted. I didn't think he would find it funny; it would be too soon. Things between us are still a little tense.

I told Parker that I would get dinner going while he was gone and that it should be almost ready when he got back. I was out getting the grill ready for steaks that we were going to have when something caught my eye in the yard. It was a little boy with a dog. What the hell were they doing in the yard? It's totally fenced and gated. I was about to say something when they ran toward the fence and went right through it and vanished. Crap! I was hoping that in the wilds here I would not run into any spirits. I am going to have to be very careful and concentrate on what I am seeing. Sometimes they look as real as me and sometime not.

Now the question is do I tell Parker about this. I think that if I do it may send him over the edge, and he would leave. I think that I will wait, being he is still adjusting to me winning the lottery.

The rest of the evening was spent going over the local maps and deciding where to start looking. There are many non-park areas we could try. We agreed to go on a scouting mission tomorrow, get a map at the park lodge and get our bearings and timing for day trips that we are planning for the first few days. We thought our best bet would be the park to start.

May 4

Today did not seem as tense between us. We were up early, had something to eat, packed lunch and were off. We made it to the lodge in the national park and got our map. We traveled, I think, every road on the map, but I'm sure we didn't. Some areas were remote, and we agreed to concentrate on the remote areas. These areas were almost like being in Alaska again. The greenery and moss is so hard to explain. It is a wonderworld of green. If BF (Bigfoot) is here this is where we should find him if we can see him or her through the trees and ferns. It is a dense old growth area. We did stop and ask if ATVs were allowed. They are allowed but only on designated roads or trails, unlike Alaska's Denali Park where it seemed we went wherever we needed to go. We have our map and found that camping is allowed.

I really had to be careful during the drive as I saw some people that Parker never noticed on the side of the road. Spirits. I did not look too closely so I am not able to give a description but the one thing I did notice was the clothing. I had to be from what little I saw from another century, and they were sort of see through.

About four we decided to call it a day and head back to the house. It is only about a thirty plus mile ride, so it did not take too long to get back.

After cleaning ourselves up and had some dinner we just sat and talked about where we would try tomorrow, just a day trip. Then there was the map. Really? You have regular roads; trails where only motorcycles are allowed and other roads/trails for ATVs. I think we will be very confused for a while. I'm sure we will unintentionally end up on something we shouldn't be on. We were able to sign up to rent ATVs for tomorrow, but they will not be available until ten a.m. Hopefully they will have a better map for us.

I hope we run into some sign or hear something. Bigfoot is known to throw rocks, screech, knock on trees among other things. We'll see tomorrow.

May 5

This was our first day trip. Thank God I brought the GPS with us. If we didn't have it, I don't think anyone would have found us as we would have run out of gas and been stranded. Oh, and the map was the map. Very hard to read and confusing.

It started off easy enough. Main roads to other roads, then sort of smaller roads and then some trails. We were not sure if we should be on some of the trails as we traveled deeper in the forest. We did know and were told not to make our own trails and we did not.

We stopped for lunch after about 2 – 2 ½ hours or so had something to eat and then started to explore. I entered our start area on the GPS and then added where we were. It was so dense that I was afraid we would never find the ATV if we walked too far away from it. We ran across what looked like a foot trail or an animal trail. We marked it with some branches so we would know where we started. The walking was not too bad on the trail, we were quiet and listening for anything unusual. Nothing but sounds of nature. No whistles, branches snaping or the feeling like we were being watched. After about another couple of hours we decided to make our way back to the ATV. That was the easy part.

Now we had to interpret the map to get back. This place needs better maps. We started by going the way we thought we came but after while things did not look familiar. We were still on one of the, we think, smaller trails that we were allowed on. We followed this for a while thinking it would lead to a road. Not, it ended. Ok, back we went. Did we miss a turn off? At this point had no clue. I fired up the GPS to see if it would help. It did sort of. It gave us a direction to go and using the map, trails and then roads we finally got back to where we started. We did not realize how long we were out there. It was almost five when we pulled into the lodge area to return the ATV's.

On the way back to the house we did not talk much. I think we were tired and intimidated by the forest and the lack of directions on the map. We were slowly realizing that we would need to be very careful or stay in one area and get familiar with it so we could find our way out.

Back at the house we cleaned up and agreed to talk after dinner with a very stiff drink.

We stayed in the house by the dining room table so we could look at the map together. We needed to decide what area we wanted to concentrate on even though we had only gone out once. We agreed that searching areas would be time consuming, hard, and somewhat dangerous. We did not want to get lost in the great expanse of the forest, GPS or not as it could be miles and miles to walk out.

We decided on an area that we estimated would take us about an hour, an hour, and a half to get to. It was close to where we were today but closer to more established trails and camping and by camping, I mean outback camping. It was remote and had a stream nearby. Once this was agreed on, I asked, suggested that maybe tomorrow we head into town to see the sights whatever they may be. Parker thought this was a good idea after the stress today and that then we could go back to the house and decide when we would take our next trip into the forest.

May 6

We decided to go into Carson first. There are three other towns a short distance away, eight to fifteen miles. We decided to try Carson first as it is basically in our back yard. It is small with a general store, some restaurants, and shops. Here is a surprise.... They have hot springs! We did not go in but walked by the place. Parker did not want to try them out. No sense of adventure.

It did not take us long to go through the town, so we continued to the next one. This was still small, but they had a real grocery store that we stopped in to pick up stuff we needed and some things we didn't.

The towns were basically the same but different, trying to draw in tourists. White Salmon was different, they had a salmon fence. By that I mean the picture of a salmon made by intertwining colors into the fence. It was really interesting and very unusual, but it worked, and it was big. I wished I had thought of bringing a camera. Maybe I can pick one up if one of the stores still carry them. Even a disposable, do they still make them?

I am not used to small towns, the towns we were in were very nice, clean, and well laid out. They all seemed to have wine stores, microbreweries, shops, and restaurants. We did stop for lunch at one of the many breweries, it was very good.

We asked around about sites to see and the most answers we got were about several waterfalls and the best hiking trails were to try. Yes, hiking is in our future but not for sightseeing.

When we got back to the house, we put our purchases away and agreed on what to have for dinner. We settled down with a drink and went over the maps again. We will make arrangements for an overnight stay in the park tomorrow. So again, this will be a day off, but still busy getting our gear together. It seems like we have been here forever, but I also realize that time is passing, and we only have about twenty more days here. We need to get serious and get moving.

May 7

I slept in this morning. What woke me up was a barking dog. Really? I don't remember a dog next door. Ok, I did not mention it earlier but there is one house close to us on one side but that is the only one.

Maybe it was all the fresh air with walking around the towns yesterday. Parker had coffee ready, he said cops live on coffee. I asked Parker about the barking and if he noticed the dog next door. He just looked at me and said that I must have been dreaming, he did not hear anything. Uh oh. Was it the dog from a few days ago with the little boy that I saw? I'll need to keep an eye out. I may even spend some time in the yard today.

We have our reservation for tomorrow. Just an overnight stay. The rest of the day we were busy packing our backpacks, making sure we had everything on our list. I'm not sure of us going out on our own. When we were in Alaska, we had a guide who provided everything. Depending on how this trip goes, I may have to talk Parker into a guide. Who knows he or she may already know an area where BF has been spotted or heard. I'll see how this trip goes tomorrow, I'm not sure about this.

The rest of our day was quiet, no dogs barking, thank you. Tomorrow should be interesting. This is going to be very different than in Alaska when everything was taken care of for us. There is something to say for guides that arrange everything, getting there, food and other stuff. Tomorrow.

May 8

We are leaving for the first overnight trip in Gifford. I decided to leave the journal here at the house, one less thing to carry.

May 9

We are back. This was not a fun adventure. It started out ok but with the maps that we hate, that does not tell us much, it took, seemed, forever to get where we wanted to be. Once there we set up our camp, got firewood and then started to explore. Initially we did not go far into the forest as it was so dense and green. We were concerned that we would not make it back. Then I remembered the GPS. Once we had that and figured out how to use it again, we were able to go out further from our camp.

We did not run into anything unusual that they talk about when trying to find a BF. No rocks piled up, no footprints, no trees broken and set in an unusual pattern, the forest seemed very quiet. Nothing. Maybe that was a sign in itself. No clue.

It was almost a comedy, the two of us trying to get a fire started and something to eat. Setting up the tent seemed to go ok. Hey, we got it up and sleeping bags into it. We sat around the fire; I think both of us were uncomfortable about sleeping in such close quarters.

Finally making it into the tent the tension broke, we laughed about it. Really two grown people having an issue about sharing a place to sleep. We got over it. The night was uneventful, and we were both up early.

The forest was still quiet. It started to freak us out a little. No birds chirping, no rustling in the underbrush of small animals. Was someone or something there watching us? I did not sense anything. No spirits that I could see so what was it? We decided to venture out again but in a different direction than yesterday. With the GPS we felt comfortable to go out a little farther. It was difficult walking through the forest. We did not find any game trails to follow which would have made things easier. That is one thing that I forgot about, game trails. We will need to try and locate them for future expeditions.

It was late afternoon when we broke camp, packed up and headed home. The first thing I did, and I think Parker did too, was to get a nice hot shower. It was getting late, and we decided to have a lite supper, a night cap and call it a day. We agreed to talk in the morning.

May 10

The first order of business after breakfast was to get our gear and go through it. We did not think anything got damaged but the tent and sleeping bags would need some fresh air. Once that was done, we decided to go over the maps again. We also talked about how quiet the forest was. Maybe this was a good place to check out again. We agreed to try this area again. Parker suggested two or three nights. He said that with as quiet as the forest was, there was something there and if we stayed a little longer it may show itself. It made sense to me. So, we agreed, and called to make reservations for the ATV's and camping for three nights but only got two nights.

We spent most of our day making a list being we would be gone longer. A trip to the store was in order for some supplies. Easy food stuff that would take no time to prepare. In other words, canned food, breakfast bars, stuff that would not spoil. One thing we needed to remember was a can opener that was not electric, like in the house. It went on the top of our list! Parker volunteered to go to the store while I started getting gear together.

Barking. The boy and dog are back. They are playing fetch in the yard. I made my way down, trying to be quiet so not to spook them. Really did I just write that. I made my way to where they would see me, but far enough away not to scare them. When the boy noticed me, he waived. I waived back. He started to approach but before he could get a little closer, he and the dog disappeared. I think and have the feeling that someone is watching over him, and they think that I may be a threat. At least I know that they see me too. I am hoping that with this thing that I have will maybe be able to help him and his dog go to where they need to be. Time will tell and I hope that I will have the time.

Parker is back. Work to be done.

May 11

Where to start. I should have brought my journal with me because now I have to write it for down three days. I am going to try and keep it in order and log what happened to the best of my memory for each day.

We made our way back to the same area. This time was a little different, birds could be heard and small animal noise in the underbrush where back. We set up camp and decided to see if we could find an animal trail. Late in the day we found a trail. We marked it on the GPS but decided not to follow it as it was getting late, and we did not want to be in the forest at night. We would never have found our way back to the camp.

Back at the camp we got our fire going and had some dinner. Just before we turned in things in the forest went quiet. We strained to hear anything. Nothing, it was un-nerving. We decided to turn in but we both knew we would be listening for anything, abnormal or unusual. I'm not sure who woke up first but suddenly we were both awake. What we heard was close but not real close, it was in the forest. It sounded like whimpering. Thank you, it wasn't just me that heard this. It was real. We whispered to each other, what in the woods would or could whimper? Was there a lost child out there? Should we go out and look? We checked the time, and it was about an hour before sunrise. We decided to wait. We did not want to get lost in the forest and thought that whoever was whimpering would still be out there and us rushing off would endanger not only ourselves but that person too if we were all lost.

May 12

Being we were already up, as soon as the sun started to show itself, we were off. Parker, being a police officer was in full search and recovery mode. It was agreed that this person, child, whatever needed to be found and brought to the authorities. But I reminded him that we could not just go in with, excuse the expressing, with guns blazing. We needed to concentrate and know where we were going so, we would know how to get all of us back safely, GPS or no GPS. We had a general direction of the whimpering we heard and headed out. We were determined to find the source, so we made sure that we had water and snacks with us. We realized on our way to where we thought the sound was coming from the whimpering had stopped. We continued hoping to see some kind of sign. Broken branches, footprints, anything.

We stumbled across an animal trail, marked it, and started to follow. One thing that we did in the past was to mark where we found the trail so that when we backtrack, we know where we started and how to get back to camp.

We followed the trail for about an hour, it was not too bad just a little slippery in spots. When we came to the slippery spots, we were very careful to look for footprints before we walked through. We really did not see anything, no sign that someone had been down the trail. We decided to go back and then check out the trail we found yesterday. The whimpering could have come from there too. Sound travels in weird ways in the forest with all the trees and vegetation around.

We got to the other trail and followed it for an hour, hour and a half, and again found nothing.

I know it was not a spirit or ghost as Parker had heard the whimpering too unless he's not telling me something. It was starting to get late, so we decided to head back to camp.

Back at camp we talked about what to do if we heard the whimpering again. Will we chance it and go out in the dark? We had good flashlights so seeing where we were going would not be a problem. We decided that if we heard it again, we would go in but not very far, just enough to figure out where it was coming from.

May 13

It was about the same time in the morning when we heard it again. We got our shoes on and grabbed our flashlights and went out. Initially we moved very slowly so we would not spook the person out there. It was hard going being there was no trail and trying not to fall over downed small trees, branches and rocks was tough. It seemed as we progressed the sound got a little louder. We followed the sound as best we could.

The sun was just coming up and we were able to see a little better. The sound seemed to dissipate as the sun came up. Was this person afraid of the dark forest and started whimpering when the dark got to be too much? We thought that we might be in the right area and slowed down. The forest was again quiet. We were looking for anything and then we saw something. It looked like a small adult curled up against a large fallen tree in dark clothing. Parker held me back and motioned to be quiet. We moved very slowly but he/she heard us, looked at us, stood up and took off faster than I have ever seen anyone run.

We just sort of stood there and then looked at each other. What? There was no way we would be able to follow he/she was just too fast. We did go and check out the area where we saw, ok – her, looking for anything she may have dropped. We found nothing. Just a really bad smell, which would make sense if they had been lost in the forest for a long period of time.

We had traveled farther than we thought and when we finally made it back to camp it was late morning. Coffee and breakfast was in our immediate future. During breakfast we decided to break camp and head back to the house. I asked if we should report the sighting of the person out there. Parker said no, that if the person wanted to be found they would not have run away from us. But something was nagging at me, I wasn't sure, I would have to think about it.

We spent the next hour or so breaking camp packing the ATVs for the ride back. Oh, and yes, the ride back was just as frustrating as before. Maybe the third time will be the charm.

Back at the house was like before, unpacking and airing everything out. One thing we did was make reservations for four nights of camping. Evidently the area we want to be in is very popular and we now have two days to kill. Sorry but this does not break my heart, I could use a day or two.

Ok, am I nuts? I am lying in bed and writing this. The person in the woods, I'm not sure if it was a person in dark clothing. I know it was not a spirit as Parker had seen it too. Maybe some sleep and a clear head in the morning will help me figure this out.

May 14

Ok, the sun was just barely up, and that damn dog is barking. I looked at the clock and it is 5:15 in the morning. I need to figure this thing out and see if I can make contact with this boy and his dog. I really, really wanted to sleep in this morning. Too late, up and the order of business right now is coffee.

Parker was still sleeping when I got up. I made coffee and took my cup to the ground level patio. I could still see the boy and his dog. They were playing in the yard and having a great time. They noticed me and stopped playing. They slowly and cautiously came toward me. I just waived. The boy waived back and inched a little bit closer; you could tell that he was unsure as to why I could see him. I did not move, just sat there with my coffee. He was in what I think was a homemade shirt and pants, no shoes.

He got closer and said hi. OMG, I think that I will be able to talk to them! I said hi back, what's your name? He said Samuel but that everyone called him Sam unless he was in trouble. I laughed at that and said my name is Sara. I asked if he was having fun with his dog, and he just smiled and petted the animal. I asked how long he has been here, and he had no idea but was hoping that his mom and dad would come for him. He said that it seemed like a really long time since he saw them but was told not to go far from here by his mom and dad before, this is where they lived and farmed. I asked what was before and he could not answer.

After watching many, many ghost hunting programs and reading up on this over the past year I asked him if he saw any kind of light. He said yes but it was farther than he should go. I asked how far, he pointed at a tree about 100 feet away. He said that it seemed like it was always there and not sure what it was. I asked him, what if your mom and dad were waiting in the light for you. You could just get a little closer and look. See if you can see them. He immediately said no. Not allowed to go that far. He then said I have to go and was gone. Crap. It seemed so easy on tv. But if I can see him again, I will keep trying. He is a real cutie, maybe six or seven years old.

I went up for more coffee, not sure how long I was down on the patio. And thank you, who do I run into, Parker. He had this weird look on his face, and I just knew. He had seen me talking to the air though I'm not sure if he heard what I was saying. I just said good morning and oh boy, now what do I do or say? Let him ask, I'll just go on like nothing out of the ordinary happened. First the lottery thing and now this. It may send him over the edge if I need to explain talking to nothing he can see.

Parker kept looking at me like he wanted to ask something but didn't. I just went on as normal. I just hope that he does not go into police mode and start watching me, like a mini stake out. Today was a real day off and we planned on doing our shopping and packing tomorrow for our camping trip on the 16th. So, it was watching tv, reading or just sitting outside. It was really relaxing and enjoyable. We both did what we wanted to do and did not feel that we had to keep each other company or entertained.

Tomorrow will be busy. The first thing will be hitting the grocery store. Until tomorrow.

May 15

Sam was out in the yard this morning. I had to run down and talk to Sam regardless of Parker. I wanted him to know that we would be gone for a few days but that we would be back. I did not want Sam to feel abandoned. I was most likely the first person in a very long while to talk to him. I think that I lucked out, Parker was in the shower when I went down. I explained to Sam that we were going on a camping trip and would be back in four days. He seemed to take the info ok. He said that he would look for me then and to have fun.

The rest of the day was packing our gear and hitting the grocery store. We have gotten pretty good at packing even though we had more stuff to pack for the four days. Thank you for ATV's or we would be feeling like pack mules. I am looking forward to tomorrow but not and I don't know why.

We had agreed that dinner tonight would be simple, less to clean up afterward and then we could look over the map again and do a little planning. I think that we both decided that finding, seeing, or hearing a BF would be by sheer luck and that all the planning in the world will not be of any help.

May 16

I'm sitting in front of our campfire. The trek in was the same as before…The maps here a really bad. I know I keep bringing it up but, they are really bad! I'm not sure how anyone finds their way around the park. Luckily, we had saved the GPS coordinates from our first trip We got here late morning and spent the afternoon setting up the camp. It took a little longer as we are staying for four nights.

So far, we have not heard anything unusual in the area, no crying, just the usual forest sounds. Tomorrow, we plan on trying to find the game trail from our first trip. Should be fun, not! Am I getting too old for this, or do I need to hit the gym when I get home? I'll figure that one out when I get back home.

 May 17

We were up early, packed some food and water along with other stuff like a flashlight, bear spray and our GPS. What can I say about trekking through a forest, granted a magical, beautiful forest looking for something that a lot of people do not believe exists. I am bord to death, Parker was taking the lead. He wanted to make sure we did not miss any sign. We had found the game trail from our first outing, marked our start again and walked about two to three hours. We stopped in a small clearing and had something to eat and drink. We decided to start back and then to check out the opposite direction from where we started. When we got back to where we started, I basically said enough. It was late afternoon and we still had three days and our walk back to the camp. Parker agreed, we would go in the opposite direction tomorrow when we are rested and fresh.

I am jotting this down. It is late or early depending on how you look at it, we heard the crying again. We are off with our flashlights.

 May 18

We are back at camp. It was a long night, not sure how much searching we will do today. We both slept in.

We grabbed our GPS and our flashlights and off we went when we heard the crying. We tried to be as quiet as possible, not easy stumbling around in a dark forest, to see if we could locate the person crying. It seemed that every time we got a little close, he or she moved away. We played this cat and mouse for about two hours when the crying just stopped. We waited for a while to see if it would start again but nothing. We made our way back to camp and fell into our sleeping bags.

We talked over some food and decided to go back to where we were last night. We wanted to see if there were any footprints, anything to give us an idea of who was out there and if we could track him/her. We got back to where we thought we were and started searching the ground for prints. Parker thought that there were a couple, but they were not clear as they were in mud, and it looked like whoever was running and the prints were smeared. The only other thing we found was some broken branches, but I didn't think that it would be unusual as there are animals moving around in the forest. One thing we did find not far from the smeared prints was a small clearing. It looked like the grass and plants had been walked on, areas where the grass was crushed down. While looking at the sight Parker stopped and said look…. It looked like the plants were fine and then not. It was like someone dropped in and started walking around. There were no pints or crushed grass opposite of where the prints started. We just looked at each other and not sure who said it, but we agreed this was weird. How do tracks just start?

It was getting late, so we made our way back to the camp. After dinner we talked about the clearing, did we miss something? We agreed that other than the area of crushed grass there was nothing there. No footprints, nothing on the ground that did not belong. We were at a loss as to what happened or what was there. We had no clue. We also decided that if we heard the crying again that we would try to catch who it was now that we are familiar with the area and hopefully could be a little quieter going through the forest.

May 19

Crap, Crap, Crap……. This was our last night, and we leave tomorrow. I cannot believe what we saw. We heard the crying and were off as soon as we heard it. It was a little easier moving through the forest as we just took the same way as the night before. The closer we got the slower we went, to make as little noise as possible. We were basically creeping through the forest when we both saw a glow. Ok, was this some night hunters or something more sinister? We both got down on hands and knees, no flashlights and crawled toward the glow. The closer we got the brighter the light and the crying got louder.

I am writing this but still cannot believe what we saw. We were not real close and did not want to get too close. What we saw, both of us had seen in the past. It was a portal. We were in shock. Standing a little way from the portal was big foot. Not one but three! One you could tell was the male, he was really large. The other two had to be the mother and a child, maybe a teenager, smaller than the male but still big. They were talking and motioning for her/him to go out into the forest. The smaller one kept holding on to what I think was mom. Finally, mom disengaged the smaller one even though it was crying. Both kept motioning to go into the forest. They seemed to be adamant but kind about it. We just sat there not moving, afraid to. We did not want to let them know we were there. Then the adults walked back into the portal, and it vanished. The child was still there and crying.

We did not move. Even if this was a teenager, it was still big and could really hurt or kill us. Slowly the child started into the forest crying the whole time. We did not move or try to follow, or talk, we just sat there. After what seemed like years the portal re-appeared. The two BF walked out and waited. After a little while the male made some calls, a whistle, and some sound I can't describe. You could hear the child running through the forest. She/he was no longer crying and the whole-body posture of her/him, sorry just cannot call it "IT," was different. She/he had something in her/his hands and seemed very proud.

The item was shown to the two adults and hugs were exchanged. Then they walked into the portal, and they were gone.

Parker and I sat there until we noticed that the sun was coming up, we were in shock. We got up, without a word, and made our way back to our camp. We did not talk on the way back or when we got back to camp. At camp we got some coffee going, cleaned up a bit and grabbed some food.

As we sat there with our coffee it finally hit us. What we saw. We both started talking at once. Did we really see what we saw? Another vortex/portal? Would they be coming back tonight? As we settled down and just sat there with our coffee. We decided to go back out today. We wanted to double check to see if there was anything that they may have dropped or if there were footprints. I asked Parker if he could see what the juvenal had in her/his hands. He said no, but now the crying made sense. How? He thought that this was some kind of a test. They had him /her go out into our world to retrieve something as a rite of passage. I sat and thought about that, and it made sense. Would they be coming back tonight? We did not think so, but we will be out there to see.

As we were getting ready to head out something hit my brain and, on our walk back into the forest, I explained to Parker about something that I just remembered reading. It was a theory about BF. They have been said to have almost magical powers, able to disappear and if that was the case it was not magic, it was a portal. It was in an article that I remembered and then I also remembered that the article mentioned that they were from a different dimension and could enter ours through a portal. Ok, this is sort of scary. You could just be walking through the forest on a nice hike and boom, a portal just opens. Then what? What if it opened exactly where you were standing, would it kill you. Is that why so many people disappear in forests, especially in Alaska? Do they take you if you are a witness to them coming into our dimension, again never to be seen? Is that what happened to Jim when he disappeared in Alaska? Jim and Marni do not talk about the time they were missing, and I don't either. I can't and I think that it is the same for them. Some experiences are better left alone and not talked about.

We got to the area and looked around. We did not see anything out of the ordinary, no footprints or anything that seemed out of place on the ground. Nothing. We decided to head back for a nap as we will be out there again tonight.

We were back at the same place, the same hiding place about the same time we noticed the light in the forest last night. We were there for about two – three hours just waiting. We finally decided to head back to camp, and we did not think they would be back. The child's search had been successful, so at this point there was no reason for them to return.

Back at camp, we got a little more sleep, packed some things that we would not need in the morning, preparing for the trip back to the lodge and then to the house in the morning.

May 20

After packing everything up in our camp, making sure we had everything and securing the stuff to the ATVs we headed back. The drive to the house was quiet as I think we were both exhausted. We unpacked the car leaving most of the stuff in the garage to be dealt with later or tomorrow. It was about one in the afternoon and both of us headed to our rooms for a hot shower and a nap.

I woke up with a start and had a hard time remembering where I was. It was a dream, and I was in a place I needed to leave but had to convince someone or something to do so and suddenly I was awake and the dream, or nightmare, quickly disappeared from my memory. What the hell was that about? I looked at the clock on the bedside table and it was an hour and a half later. I got up and wandered into the main living area and out to the deck. I was hoping to see Sam so that he would know that we were back, but no luck. I'll just have to wait for his dog to do some barking.

Parker joined me about a half hour later, and we went to the garage to deal with all our stuff. Better today than tomorrow. We are taking tomorrow off and agreed not to really talk about what we saw until then. We both needed it to sink in.

The rest of the evening was quiet, and we both turned in early. What a couple days!

May 21

We were both up early today. It is amazing what a good night's sleep on a real mattress and not the ground will do for a person. Over breakfast we talked, we only had about nine days left on our trip and after what we saw, how could we top that? We decided to take today and tomorrow off. We needed to completely re-charge. We did agree to go back into the woods but a different area.

Our camping stuff was dealt with yesterday so we would just need to pack up again when we were ready to leave.

It seemed like we were ignoring the elephant in the room or should I say Bigfoot. I decided not to bring it up until lunch, we could relax and then talk.

Lunch was nice until Parker brought up what we had seen in the woods. He wanted to know if that is what I saw while in the portal in Alaska. I told him that I really could not say as my memory of the time I was in there is sort of missing. I only have very vague memories of the time I was in there, shadows of things, images. Nothing I could describe. I don't think he believed me as he started to get a little PO'd at me. I asked him why would I lie about this? I was just as surprised at what happened as he was.

I said, "do you know how lucky we are to have seen that." Then the truth sort of came out. He said that if I could remember and if we had a camera, we would be millionaires, combining both of our stories, trips, together. I just sort of looked at him. Was I hearing what I thought I was hearing? I asked him if that was the only reason, he wanted to do this trip was to try and prove BF existed, to prove it and make money. What he said next really hurt and shocked me. I did not think he could be so cruel. He said that he was hoping to have a sighting and to possibly document it, but he forgot a camera and was not sure how I would react if he purchased one and brought it out with us. He thought that I would get suspicious. He wanted to get real evidence. But he did not have it even though he had done his own searches in Alaska. He said that he could still write a book about it. He said that I could help him as his eyewitness and maybe a co-author and that the book would be a best seller. He said that he could go into town and get a camera and then we could go out, back to the area for a day and take pictures of the area, especially the area where the portal appeared. Then he could pay for trips like this on his own and for me to possibly come with him.

He did not say this but the only thing I could think of was that he wanted me to be his sidekick.

Why couldn't he just be honest with me from the beginning, that he wanted to find proof of BF. Write a book, become famous. If he had a plan, tell me up front? Anything would be better than this.

I was so mad; God was I mad. How could I have been so wrong? I felt used. If he had been honest with me from the beginning, I may have gone along with it. I also would most likely not have told him about the lottery win. I would have just made something up about how I was paying for the trip. I had a hard time controlling myself, but my temper took over. I told him that the only reason I told him about the lottery win was because he questioned and nagged me about how I was paying for this. That I trusted him with that information. That I did not want him to think I was going into debt. I thought that he would be happy for me not resentful. That I should have told him it was none of his business. It now seemed to me that all he wanted to get out of this trip was money and fame, I was done! He could get a camera and go out there himself. He tried to say something, but I cut him off. I screamed, I AM DONE, TRIP OVER! I told him that he could change his airline ticket to leave sooner or stay being we had two cars and that the house was paid for through the next seven days. He could do whatever he pleased. I told him to say away from me that I was going to make arrangements to leave as soon as possible. That I will be calling my travel agent to see what the earliest, quickest flight home was. I then stormed to my room to pack and call my travel agent.

There were no flights that I could make today, the best Amy could do was for tomorrow at three. It will be late when I get back home, but I don't care.

I went down to the kitchen to get a sandwich and a drink. Parker was nowhere to be found, hopefully he is hold up in his room. I decided to go down to the patio and try to relax. Parker had never made his way down here so I was not worried that he would. While I was there Sam and his dog appeared. I said hi, how are you doing today? He said fine. I asked if he thought about the light, we talked about what he sees, would he be interested in getting a little closer if I walked with him. I did not want to tell him that I was leaving tomorrow. He thought about it and asked if we could go slow. I told him that I would walk as slow as he wanted me to and that if he wanted to stop it was all up to him. He said ok.

We started to walk in the direction he led me to. I could not see the light. Sam was very cautious and did not move fast. His dog was right next to us, like he knew where he was going and who he would see. Sam and I chatted about his family and how much he missed them. He suddenly slowed and I stopped. The dog was so excited, running from Sam to something I could not see. I was not sure how close we were to the light, so I took my clue from the dog. I knelt down on my knees and would have put my arm around him but didn't think that would work. I quietly asked him what do you see? He said, with wonder in his voice, that it was his mom and dad. They wanted them to come to them. He turned and looked at me and said that he was afraid. I asked why? He said that he had been gone so long he must be in trouble. I looked at him and told him that they are thrilled to see him and that they have been waiting a long time for you, because they love you. He looked at me and then the dog, who was also happy to see them but would not leave Sam's side. He missed the whole family too but would stay with Sam no matter what. Sam looked at me and asked if I would be ok if he wanted to go to them. I said that I would miss him, remember him but that is where he needed to be with his mom, dad, and his dog. Suddenly he and the dog were running, and then they were gone.

I'm not sure if it was a release of all the anger I felt or that a little boy was reunited with his family, but for the second time in my life I just sat down and sobbed. Happy for Sam and so sad about Parker.

I made my way back in, thank you, no sign of Parker. I plan on leaving early tomorrow even though my flight is in the afternoon. I'll spend my time in the airport. I'll buy something to read and take my mind off this trip. I am going to leave a note for Parker to do whatever he wants with the gear. Take it home and use it, donate it, or throw it out. I don't care. I am turning in early as I am mentally exhausted. First

Parker and then the emotions I felt when Sam found his family.

May 22

I was up early, about four in the morning. I had already packed and had my clothes laid out for my trip home. I can't believe that I am still so angry and hurt. I tried to be quiet as I showered and got ready to leave. I held my breath as I thought I heard Parker moving about, but it was not him, hopefully just my imagination and not another spirit.

As I was coming in from putting my luggage into the car I ran right into Parker. He wanted to know what I was doing, why was I up so early, he thought that someone had broken in when he heard someone walking around so early. I told him that it was no concern of his and that as I said yesterday this trip is over you can do whatever you want for the rest of your time here. I told him that I left a note on the counter and that I was going to the airport, I was going home. He wanted to know if we could talk about yesterday and I told him in no uncertain terms no. I was still way to hurt and angry and that I was out of here. I walked past him, grabbed my purse and carryon, and went to the car.

I'm on the plane writing this. I am having second thoughts. Did I overreact? No. I think that once he learned that I had won the lottery, even though I did not tell him how much, he figured out that I could finance and help him to make money on me and my sisters story attaching this trip to the story if we found anything. The sad thing is that I don't think it was his first thought at the beginning of our trip, it just sort of morphed in his brain.

I think that I will be glad to get home, put this whole thing behind me and figure out what to do next. I feel like the world has opened up since I helped Sam and his dog go home to his parents. I can talk to them! Maybe that is what I need to do is find areas that are interesting, go see them, not necessarily to find spirits to help, but hey if I run into someone who is lost why not help.

May 23

I am home. I got in late last night and just fell into bed. First things first this morning – coffee and something to eat as I had not had much at the airport or on the plane, luckily, I had a frozen breakfast thing in the freezer. Not great but filled the void. The next order of business was unpacking and laundry. I was restless and felt that I needed to put things right, where they belonged.

I still can't believe Parker. I think that I am over my anger but the disappointment in him remains. How could I have been so wrong, at least he did show his true colors before I got in too deep. I was starting to have feelings for him, and I was hoping to put something to him if this trip went well. I wanted to hire him to travel with me to different locations to see what we could see and possibly let him know that I could see spirits. We would have made a good team with his training as a cop. He would have been great looking into the history of the places we would visit.

I am excited about the spirits. They could help to solve mysteries and hopefully get the answers they need and move on. Helping Sam and his dog was the best thing ever, along with what we saw in the forest. I still can't believe that I know BF comes from another dimension. Who would believe me if I told them? No one. They, whoever they are, would want proof that I don't have and glad that I don't.

I am going to have to think about what's next for me. But for right now grocery shopping is in my immediate future along with picking up my mail and cancelling the hold. Back to normalcy.

The rest of today and tomorrow will be catching up on bills, phone messages and just relaxing.

May 24

Ok, bills mailed, messages answered, groceries purchased and put away and I just can't sit still. I think Parker is on my mind. The anger is gone but I feel like I have lost something. After talking for a year or a little more I trusted him. I thought that he would be happy for me not resentful that I divulged winning the lottery to him. I am very careful with that info; most people do not know that I won and that is how I like it and live my life. Thank God, I did not tell him how much. Looking back there was a subtle change. He did not seem like his old self. It was like he was holding back. The connection between us was there but not, not like in Alaska. What really hit me was remembering him saying that he would be able to pay for trips like this on his own and for me to come with him. Why does it always come down to money? I guess if you have it, you have a different perspective to those that don't and want it or is it just a man thing?

I know that I just got home but I need something to fill the days. I think that I will surf the net and see if any locations or places interest me.

It was early evening. Parker showed up on my doorstep. Initially I thought how did he find me? Then I remembered he sent my sister's diary to me. I should get a PO box. He is currently, hopefully, sleeping in my guest room. With my anger gone I invited him in, what else was I supposed to do? Slam the door in his face, regardless of what happened we had a history. He said that he wanted to apologize and to talk.

Parker was nervous when I invited him in. I took his coat and motioned to the back of the house where the kitchen and family room were. I asked if he wanted something to drink and he declined. I said that before we got talking, I needed to order my dinner. I was ordering pizza; did he want anything special on it or was there something he did not like? He said not to worry about him, he was fine. I told him that my anger was gone and that I would not eat in front of him and if we were going to talk, he would share a pizza and have a drink. He said anything would be fine on the pizza. He asked if I had bourbon. I said yes and poured one for both of us.

I had the tv on and we just sat there in a very uncomfortable silence. I did not want to start the conversation; I wanted him to. He was the one who just showed up on my doorstep and I am sure he should be back in Alaska.

The pizza came, another drink and it started to feel like before, in Alaska. It initially seemed like the old Parker was back, but it was too soon to tell. What did he want to talk about?

Pizza done, leftovers put away, another drink poured, tv on a low volume for noise, Parker started talking. The first thing he did was apologize. He said that he was surprised and shocked when I told him that I had won the lottery. He had figured that I had old money not that I had won a major prize and could do just about anything I wanted to do, money no object. He said that the green-eyed monster, envy, had reared its head but he had held it together, for a time. Yes, he realized that he was treating me differently, but not by much. He said that, yes, he did want to go find BF to find proof, once and for all, and turn that proof into something financially beneficial to him.

He said that after my blow up at the house and me leaving made him think about what he was doing, trying to do, and that it was just not right. He was not brought up to use people and that is what he was trying to do.

I accepted his apology and we just sat there for a while, not really saying anything. I asked him where he was staying for the night. He stated that he would need to find a hotel as he had come straight from the airport. He wanted to know if there was anything in the area. I said no, nothing. This was strictly a residential area. I told him to get his things that I had a guest room available if he wanted it. He said yes, thank you, that it was getting late and was exhausted mentally and physically. My guest room is always ready so when he brought his stuff in, I showed him to it and said good night.

I have no idea where our next conversation will go. I'm a little leery, is he still trying to get something from me? I don't think I should bring up him working for me. Not after his reaction to me winning the lottery. I am not looking forward to the morning.

May 25

I was up early. I did not sleep well, nightmares of being chased through the forest and wondering about today, how would things go? While I was showering, I decided to take this one minute at a time if need be. I need to get back to myself with Parker, force it if necessary. OK head up, positivity up front, here I go.

What a disappointment. Parker was not in the kitchen. I went and checked his room, and the door was still closed so he was still sleeping or getting ready for the day. I decided to make breakfast. While making breakfast a thought hit me. What if he really wanted to write a book but had no idea of a direction and he just went with the finding the BF thing. He was thinking that it would be a best seller immediately. Wrong. The world would crucify him without proof. I need to think this through before I talk to him. Halfway done Parker showed and I handed him a cup of coffee.

Parker thanked me and we had breakfast. I asked what his plans were. He said that he would be heading to the airport as he had a flight home at two and he did not want to inconvenience me any further.

I think that I surprised him by asking if he could postpone his flight by a couple days, that I had an idea but needed some time to think it through. He just sort of looked at me and asked, “are you sure”.

Should he get a hotel somewhere? No hotel, he could stay here. I just needed some time to get my thoughts together and map things out in my brain and on paper. He said that he would call and re-schedule his flight but needed to be back in Alaska in three days. I told him that would work and should be enough time.

I told him to make himself at home and left him in the kitchen and then went into my office to think this through and make notes.

I wanted to ask him some hard questions: Are you interested in writing or was the BF thing just about fame and money. If you are serious about writing? Have you ever tried to write something? A book, short story, an article? Would it be something real/factual and if so, how would you document it? Would you have the time and funds to document it? I was thinking about asking these questions, letting him think about them and then proposing that he write fiction, that is if he really wants to write. I have no idea if he has any talent for writing, maybe he thinks he does. If so, he/we may find out depending on how this goes.

I decided to wait until this evening to ask my questions, maybe this was being cruel, not sure but I wanted to make sure I had all the questions.

Why a book on BF, did the idea hit you, causing a sensation and then overnight fame?

Have you done any writing in the past, other than police reports? If so, what?
If you do want to write, would you consider something else like fiction? (I have an idea)
How much time would you be able or willing to put into writing?
If I can help, will you accept it? (not financially)
If you are serious about writing and really want to do this, can you maybe take a leave of absence to give you time to see if this is a direction you want to go in or try?

Coming up with questions was not as easy as I thought it would be. Having these and hopefully talking to Parker more will come up. I think I'll give him a list of my questions and suggest that he look them over, think on them and then we can talk tomorrow morning.

May 26

Yesterday was good. Parker took the list and said that he would review it later and thought it would be a good idea to think about the questions and then talk today. He said that he may also come up with questions. I am hoping that some of the questions do not piss him off and we start at each other again, because yesterday it seemed like we were getting back to normal.

When Parker came into the kitchen, he seemed ok, not angry or ticked off. He asked for some coffee and sat down. He wanted to talk.

Before he could say anything, I asked what he thought of my questions.
He told me that yes, he does write but was not having much success, he said that he has had several rejection letters, that the publishers did not seem interested in another book about a cop, but that they liked his style. He said that he was not good at trying to put a mystery or a crime into his writing, even with his experiences as a cop. He thought that finding and possibly documenting Bigfoot would be something publishers would jump on. He did not think of the possibility of fame, but after thinking about what he wanted to find, verifying the existence, and writing about it, it was not something he wanted. The possibility of his privacy with a discovery that big, and the park would be inundated with tourists and thought about the damage that could be done to the park. The other thing he said was, even though we know Bigfoot is real, he decided that he did not want to be responsible for destroying one of the world's mysteries.

Parker said that he had a confession, he wanted to get out of policing. He was tired and wanted to do something else. He said that in college he had taken writing classes, but life had gotten in the way. He did not elaborate, and I did not ask.

He sat back, looked at me and asked, "What were you thinking why the questions?"

All this surprised me, and I needed time to digest it. I said let me get some breakfast going, then I'll explain over breakfast. I told him that I was starving.

Over our breakfast I said that I was surprised that he wanted to get out of police work and a little more surprised that he wanted to write. I told him that I had an idea. Rather than trying to prove BF is real why not write fiction? Take what happened to us and write about it. In making it fictional event/story there would be no scrutiny. You would not be forced to prove anything but, yet you would know it was real. I have often heard that a writer should write about what they know. The police stories did not work out, but this might. Not only that but there are so many mysteries in Alaska you could write about. Go back to where it started.... Go back to Alaska.

I went on to say that I would be happy to help, but not financially. I would be willing to be his sounding board and that between the two of us, each remembering what happened, he could come up with, what I think would be a great story. He looked at me and asked what would be in it for me. I said nothing, just would like to help and did not want any credit or even being mentioned as a co-author or source. He then asked if he could use my journal from the trip. I said no. There are personal thoughts in it and that it was not for anyone but me. He seemed to accept that answer and said that he thought my idea was good, but he would need to think it over.

The day went on, and things seemed somewhat normal between us. Parker said that he would be leaving first thing in the morning as he had an early flight home and had to drop the car off at the airport.

May 27

Parker left early this morning. He thanked me for everything and said that he would be in touch. He had a lot of thinking to do about our conversation yesterday. I said that you have my number, call anytime, but remember the time difference between here and Alaska!

It will be interesting to see if he takes my suggestion to heart or not. It's his decision, his life. Only time will tell.

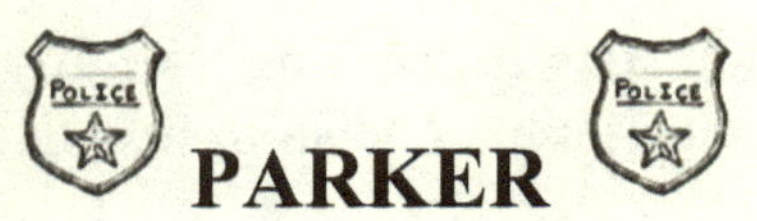

PARKER

May 28

Well, I'm back home and back to work tomorrow, even though I should still have a few days off. I got in late last night and there was a message from my boss asking if I was back from my trip and if I could come in. I called him and said sure. I've been trying to keep busy all day. Unpacking, laundry and getting my fridge stocked. I do not want to keep going over the disastrous ending of my trip with Sara. I was surprised that she did not slam the door in my face when I was on her doorstep. I needed to apologize and had the time to do it in person. I did not expect her to be as gracious as she was, letting me stay at her place. I need to send Sara an email thanking her for letting me stay at her place rather than a hotel.

There was one thing that I didn't think I could ask her about while I was at her place. It was the day she went off on me. I was looking to talk to her when I saw her in the yard. She did not see me as she had her back to me, and I was above her on the balcony. It looked like she was talking to someone or something. Was she still that pissed that she had to vent to herself? But then why did she drop to her knees and sob? I backed into the house so she would not know I was there. Was it just a release of her anger/disappointment in me? I'm curious about that incident, for some reason I don't think it was just her venting. My cop senses say it was something, but I have no idea what. One day when I think we are back to our old selves, I'll ask her, until then it will remain a mystery.

I must admit that I was a real asshole and that I fucked up big time wanting her to back me on writing a true story about our Bigfoot experience and seeming to make it all about fame and money. Maybe it was the way I presented it, hell I don't know. But she definitely went off on me and, I think, in a way it was deserved.

I really like this woman; she's feisty and knows what she wants and how to get things done. It's a dangerous combination, at least for me. I will need to be very careful if the book comes to be and I ask for her help with remembering our travels.

What no one knows and I did not share with Sara is that I'm already a published author. Just a few mystery/cop stories all taking place in Alaska. I don't publish under my name as I rely on my job as a detective for a lot of the stories and to pay the bills. They are loosely based on some of my cases with enough changes to make them fiction. They are not best sellers but had decent sales without a lot of promotion. I told Sara that I tried to publish but that no one was interested but that one agent/publishing house liked my style. At least that was not a lie, they did like my style.

I need to think about her suggestion for the book. A story but written as fiction, something that I already know how to do. Take some real details, change some things around and poof….you have a story. Fiction. I think I like the idea, I need to think on it. This could be a real opportunity and might do better than the cop stories.

May 29

Why, why the hell did I agree to go back to work early when I still, technically, had another four days of vacation? God, I hate this job. I still have a hard time trying to understand why people treat each other the way they do. Alaska has all kinds of tourists that visit, just flying in or arriving on cruise ships. Little do they know that Alaska has one of the highest crime rates. Robberies, assaults, murders. I am tired of dealing with it. Fifteen years is more than enough. I want out and if what I am thinking and planning will work, I'll be able to get out of this line of work sooner than I hoped.

It's been a rough day and I need to decompress. Dinner, a drink and back to the f'n mayhem tomorrow.

May 30

In between cases, paperwork and inspecting crime scenes I think I have it. I am excited about this. Not only do I want to write about my Washington experience, but I'm also thinking, a series of books, starting with Marni. I still have a copy of Marni's journal, which would be the starting point. I could then go on to Sara trying to find her sister, Marni, and then the Washington trip. I would change the names and possibly locations. This could work! Come up with a main character for all the travels….me? They say you should write about what you know, and I have lived it.

I need an outline for the first book and then work on the others when I have time. Once I have that I can contact Becky, my agent, and see what they think about the idea. Not sure about them as it will be out of the ordinary with what I write now. I'm hoping they will like my pitch, I'm excited about this, and I have not been excited about anything in a long time. But then…. what do I do after three? That is all I have, and I need something to base my book(s) on. I'll worry about that when the time comes. This is one Hell of an idea, and it will not be just another cop story. I am thinking and hoping my agent will like the idea as much as I do.

June 2

The past two days have been hell. We had three murders and multiple assaults to deal with. Two of the murders were by family members and fairly easy to solve. It is usually jealousy or money problems that sends people over the edge. I just don't understand "if I can't have you no one can." Divorce is not easy but murdering your spouse or boyfriend/girlfriend destroys more than one life. I don't think I will ever understand it and if I ever do start to understand it then I'm in trouble.

The paperwork never ends with these incidents. Written reports, forms to request info, keeping notes and then making sense out of them as they are taken on the fly and need to be added to more reports. It seems like fifty percent of my time is on reports and requests for information. Ok, enough of this crap. I need to think positive. I have a plan and if I am right, my days on the force will be numbered. I have a hunch that the book will be a success, if my agent goes for it.

Thankfully, I have the next two days off and I plan on working on the outline for the first book. The outline should not take too long to pull together. Just a few paragraphs to give him a quick overview of the new book. It will be interesting to hear what he has to say as this is not my usual scum of the earth bad guys and cops.

I emailed Sara this about my idea for a series, starting with her sister's story, then hers and then ours. I told her that I still had a copy of Marni's journal and that I would be using that as a guide for the first book. I did tell her that I would change names and possibly location so there would be no chance of anyone putting two and two together. The only people who would be able to do that would be the guides Marni used and they would not come forward as she disappeared on their watch. As for our story of finding Marni and her friend Jim, again, I think it would be a slim chance that any one of them would read it and if they did? Who would believe them if they came forward and said it was all real? Saving someone from a portal? They would be laughed out of the state. It will be interesting to see what Sara has to say.

June 3

Sara got back to me today. She loved the idea of a series. She asked if I would send her the outline or some pages. She is excited and curious about how I will be putting the story together. I emailed her back and said sure. I'm not going to mention that I will also be sending the outline to my agent. I have been working on it all day and I think I will get it to Sara and my agent this evening. I am hoping that my agent likes this idea and the idea of a series. Keeping my fingers crossed. I'll be on pins and needles waiting for her response.

I think Sara was waiting for my email with the outline. I has only been about an hour since I sent it and she has already gotten back to me. I wish my agent was that fast. She really liked it and would love to read any pages I would be willing to send her. She also mentioned that she would be willing to help in any way such as comparing notes for the next two books. I made a point of not asking for her journal even though it would give me a different perspective. I'm certain she would have said NO.

I just had a thought. If my agent likes the idea and the outline, I may take a leave of absence to work on the book. Even though it would be risky financially, I do have a good savings account balance and I have the proceeds from the sale of my books that I have not touched. I need to seriously consider this and push numbers to see if it is possible. I was thinking maybe a couple of months. I want to get this going as soon as possible. If my agent can't place the idea with my current publisher then I'm sure she will send it out to other publishing houses. There has to be one out there that will think the book will be successful.

June 4

Still no word from my agent.

But that's ok. I have been writing and it seems to be easier than the other books. I just can't type fast enough. I like how the story comes together. I have about two chapters already written and a ton of notes. When I stopped for lunch, a thought hit me, which is totally out of character for me. For the second book I'm thinking of adding in some romance between the two main characters. That would be me and Sara. I wonder what Sara would think about that. Yea, get real. I do like her, but I'm not sure if adding a romance would be good for me, but I think it would be good for the book.

I pushed the numbers. A leave is possible. I know my boss will not be happy since I just got back, but I have to do this. I think the best course of action will be to talk to HR first. That will be the first thing on my agenda tomorrow. I plan on giving them at least a month's notice, that I will be taking two months off. You can bet that I will be counting the days and if the book takes off, like I think it will, I can resign.

Ok, enough for now. I want to get a couple more pages done before dinner, relax and then, unfortunately, back to hell tomorrow.

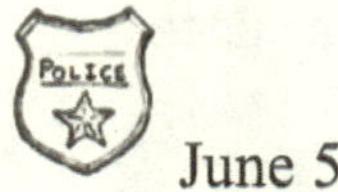

June 5

Talk about an eventful day! First HR said no problem on the leave. Though they did stress that it would be unpaid. I can live with that. I gave them the date, the end of the month to start and requested two months. I asked if they would notify the boss and got a resounding NO. That is your job, good luck!

The chief was not happy. He knew something was up when I asked to talk to him privately. Thank God the door was closed, and no one could make out what he was yelling about. He tried to guilt me into putting off the leave then demanded to know why needed a leave. I told him that the leave was for personal reasons and left it at that. Then the questions to try and get me to talk. Like I have not used that in interrogations myself, getting the person to give up info without realizing. Then it got insulting, he said that it could not be for mental health as I was just off for about a month. I did not respond at all to that one as I knew he was trying everything in the book to get me to talk.

After he settled down, he wanted to know when it would start and for how long. I gave him the info and told him that I would try not to leave a lot of cases up in the air. He said he knew that. Then he surprised me by telling me that I was one of the best detectives he has served with in a long time. He also mentioned that my co-workers and my partner most likely will not be happy as my taking a leave will increase their workload. He told me to tell Frank, my partner, in private. He would be informing everyone else at our weekly meeting tomorrow and then wished me luck with Frank.

We were called out to a very nasty domestic. The wife was taken to the hospital and the outcome looks bleak. After the interviews with witnesses, the husband was located at a local bar and was taken into custody and transported to jail. I mentioned to Frank about lunch and that it would be on me. I think he knew something was up.

Frank was not happy. He was downright pissed, and I can't blame him as he pointed out I just got back from a month off. Then he got serious and wanted to know if I was sick. I wanted to tell him yes, I was sick, but not physically sick, sick of the job. I knew I could not tell him the real reason, so I told him that I was not sick, that there was just something personal that I needed to do and that it would take time. I said that hopefully I could tell him in the future but not now. I have to give him credit. He dropped the subject but let me know that if I needed help, he would be there for me. I was touched by that as he is one of the few people who know my history.

This happened when I was about ten years old. It was just my dad, my mom and me. I don't know any of the details, but I found out much later that my mom had some mental problems. She ended up killing my dad and almost killed me. She was convicted and sentenced to life. She tried to contact me as a kid and the authorities let me know, but I wanted nothing to do with her. The police department in Portland tried to help and support me as best they could, being I did not know of any relatives at the time and ended up in the system. A couple of the officers tried to stay in touch, but life got in the way and was moved around a lot. I got tough mentally and physically bouncing from one foster home to the other and when old enough entered the military. That was not for me. I knew that I was not a lifer and got out when I could. I was still stationed in Alaska at that time and just stayed. The military had taught me what I needed, discipline and that experience helped me enter the police force. I never forgot the officers that tried to help when I was a kid and that is most likely why I ended up in law enforcement.

How did I get on this flipping subject? Oh, yea, talking about Frank.

The best news is….. wait for it, wait for it……. my agent emailed and called!!!!! She ran the outline by her boss along with the idea of additional books, which is how much she liked it and it is a GO!!!! She sent the outline to my current publisher, and they liked the idea of the book's premise and that it would be a series! They are actually drawing up a contract for three books and will have the first review of any additional books after that. Becky said that I should receive a copy of the contract in a couple weeks after she reviewed it and also suggested that I get an attorney to review it too. Becky mentioned that she would send me some names of attorneys to check out. She also congratulated me!! I am having a hard time believing this…I need an attorney! HOLY SHIT…. A CONTRACT FOR THREE BOOKS!!!! HOLY SHIT!!!

I need to email Sara and let her know the good, no GREAT NEWS!

I am going to keep working on the book when I can but, I'm definitely looking forward to my leave. Only about 29 days to go. I think that with the way my writing is going, I will almost finish the book before the 29 days are up. Then I'll have time to go over it, doing my own edits before I send it in.

It is late and I unfortunately will be back to work tomorrow.

June 6

Today was a real crapy day. Attempted murders, robberies, assaults and then all the f'n paperwork to deal with. I think I got used to being off when I was with Sara in Washington State. I forgot that this job is not necessarily nine to five. I'm very tempted to hand in my resignation and not wait to see how the book does.

There are some good points: I can concentrate on the book, no more murder and mayhem to put up with, not to mention the ton of paperwork daily. I am also considering having these books published under my real name not my pen name. The other thing that I can think of is that with fifteen years on the force, come retirement age I will still get something, but not full retirement benefits, pro/con?

I can come up with only one real negative…If I do resign and the book does not do well, then what would I do? It would be risky, especially financially.

I don't have anyone to talk to about this as most people don't know my history and that family is nonexistent or that I have published books under a pen name. Ok, big problem. I never told Sara that I was published and if I decide to ask her opinion, I may have to come clean and clue her in about my history and my existing books. I think the safest thing with Sara is to ask her opinion about resigning now rather than later. This will take a phone call not an email. Speaking of emails, I need to see if Sara got back to me about my news.

She is thrilled for me. She wanted to know if she could help in any way, to just let her know. This would be too much to explain in an email. I have her number here somewhere. I need to give her a call. She is three hours ahead of us so, it's nine-thirty her time. I don't think it would be too late to call. Hey, take a chance. Maybe that should be my new motto!

I think that I need to tell her that our trip to Washington State, even with my fuck up and her going ballistic on me was the best thing. Look what it has led to! I would never have thought of this if I had not gone to her place after Washington to apologize. Right now, I think I love that woman. Find her number!

I talked to Sara for about two – two and a half hours. It was great talking to her. She was thrilled about the contract and was surprised when I brought up leaving the force. She agreed with me about the pros and cons of leaving the force but said the decision was mine to make. She suggested that I don't make any rash decisions and take time to think it over. She also mentioned that the travel bug has hit her, and would I mind if she came out to see me in about a month from now. She said that she would try to stay out of trouble and would help with the book in any way she could and would be staying at the same hotel in Anchorage she stayed in the last time she was here. I said absolutely yes. Sara said that she would talk to her travel agent and set it up for, say an arrival on July 7th, after the holiday. I told her that would work and that we would have much more to catch up on then. She also mentioned possibly getting together with Mike and his parents, a dinner in town maybe. I told her that I would check with Mike and see what he and his parents say.

Ok, this is getting scary. The book deal and now Sara is coming out to see me! I wonder, is she attracted to me as much as I am to her? Or, like she said just has the travel bug or feels that she owes me something after the fiasco in Washington? I'll need to be on my best behavior when she is here, I am just starting to understand how attracted I am to her.

Back to the real world and my life changing decision. Sara was right, give the resignation thing time, really think it over. Wait and see what the contract says, I need more info. Though if I had to make my decision now, I would resign in a New York minute.

June 10

This work week has been hell. Won't go into it here. It's bad enough that I live it five plus days a week. I haven't written much as work has, as I said been hell. By the time I got home I was wiped physically and emotionally. Thank you, I have a couple days off unless something big comes up. I plan on writing and relaxing and hopefully get in touch with some of the names Becky gave me, but I have questions.

The only bright spot this week is Becky came through with names of attorneys specializing in contracts for authors. I haven't had much time this week to contact them, but I need to get going as I hope to have the contract from Beck sometime next week. Currently I have just been given a simple contract, that I can understand, for each book published. I have never needed an attorney, and this may be big with Becky recommending that I get an attorney. My gut back then with my first book and Becky taking it on was the right one, I had the feeling that she was honest in the beginning and would not steer me wrong and do what was best for me. I truly believe that I am published because of her. I wonder if she will up her commission. If she does, she is well worth it.

I emailed Becky some questions and I am hoping that she will get back to me before she receives the contract. I also asked her if there was a time frame to have the contract reviewed by an attorney, signed, and returned.

What the hell, was she sitting on her email, or does she not have a life? She got back to me almost immediately. She said that the contract and the cover letter will each have a time frame or deadline to return the signed documents. She answered my other questions and gave me an inside tip of attorneys she has dealt with but told me to contact at least three to four to get a feeling for them as I would most likely be working with them for quite a while. Holy crap…this is getting real! This may now, ok don't jinx it, be my new profession! God, I hope so with all my being!

Enough of this for now. Time to send out emails to the attorneys. Let's see what happens.

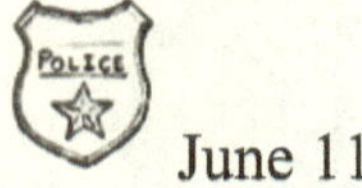

June 11

Becky's name must hold a lot of weight. I emailed four attorneys last night and at eleven this morning and I had gotten email responses from all of them. Not only just responses but details of their charges and what they would do for me. Don't these people sleep? Or are they desperate for business? Or did they check with Becky to see if I was on the up and up? I think I will be on the net most of this morning,

I have some research to do on the companies and the people.

Ok, research done. I have picked who I think is the best for me. I want to email Becky and see what she thinks about my choice, a second opinion. I emailed Becky my choice: for my attorney, George Pollock. Hopefully, she gets back to me faster than she did about the outline I sent. Though she did get it to the publisher, so time well spent but the waiting was not fun.

Becky did get back to me fast! She thought that I made the right choice in an attorney. I told her that I would contact George Pollack and find out what the next steps would be to hire him.

Emails sent and it is late afternoon. I know I should sit down and write but I think a break is in order. I think I'll pick up something for an early dinner and just take this evening off. Unfortunately, back to hell tomorrow. I was supposed to be off but one of the other detectives is out with the flu and they asked if I would cover. I'm a softy, no not, just helping out my fellow cops. Now thinking about this, I think that I will miss them. They are my substitute family. They care about me as I care about them.

If I do decide to resign, I'm not sure if they will be pissed or happy for me. Most likely both.

June 13

Again, another rough few of days…won't even go into it here. I just want to decompress. The good news is the attorney got back to me. He has agreed to represent me. Becky said that she would have a contract to me with in a day or two and to review it myself and have my attorney if I have one, review it. I emailed her back and said that I do have an attorney and gave her his name and contact info.

The attorney was a bit easier as he will not have a contract but quoted me his hourly rate to review the contract and holy shit that got my attention. $350 an hour!!!! He mentioned that if I or he feels that I may need more of his services we could then talk about a retainer. I asked about his turnaround time to review the contact. He said that if it was Carson Publishing's standard contract it would only take a day or two. I said what!? A day or two at $350 an hour?! He laughed and said no, it did not take that long, most likely an hour or two. The day or two timeline he gave me is his estimate of when he would be able to get to it and then back to me. Ok, I can breathe again. He asked if I had an estimated date to receive it and I told him the week of the 20th. I mentioned that Becky Sims with Carson Publishing would be sending him a copy of the contract as well to me. He said that he would look for her email and that he had worked with her in the past. He did not foresee any problems or issues. He said that he has reviewed several contracts from her and her company and that they tended to be straight forward. He said that he would confirm with both of us upon receipt of the contract. After reviewing it, if he had any questions or issues with it, he would first talk to me. I thanked him and made sure he had all my contact info.

This is really real!!!!!

June 19

If I haven't been at work I've been trying to write, but not getting much done. By the time I get home, have a little something to eat I have been falling into bed and then starting the whole thing over again. The only good news is that I finally had a chance to check my email and both contracts are in ahead of schedule. George confirmed receipt of it and said he would get back to me in a few days. The other good news is that I am off tomorrow. I'm not going to try and review them tonight.....same as the past few days...something to eat, a drink and bed. I'll have fresh eyes tomorrow.

June 20

I reviewed the contract from Carson Publishing first. If I am reading this right, I can give my notice! Not only that but for the second and third books, if the first does well they will be upping the royalties with each book along with the contracted amount for the other two books if sales quotas are reached for each.

Reviewing the contract from Becky was more difficult. Not sure what all the percentages in the contract mean or equal to monetarily. I will send him a copy of this one and hopefully get clarification from George.

This will work out perfectly. I only have about two weeks until my leave. If I have to give them another week or two I will, I think I owe them that. When I get back to work tomorrow, I'll be putting my two weeks' notice in. I am so looking forward to getting out of the job I call HELL, but will miss my co-workers, my family. Ok, get real buddy, don't jump the gun! Before I can do that, I need to hear George's opinion on the contracts. I'll email him and ask if he could call me with his thoughts rather than email. I want to get this going as soon as possible.

Even though I haven't had a lot of time to write, I think it is going well. I just keep chipping away, sentence by sentence when I have time to write. I have another two chapters done. When I leave/resign, I'll have more time. I plan on going over what I have written first. The last two chapters were done in such a rush; I feel that I need to review it. Soon I'll have time!

June 21

George called. I had to call him back as we were on a call, not a nice one, but at least no one died. When I was able to get back to him, his secretary said he was in a meeting and would get back to me. Tag your it, George!

When George called back, I was able to take the call. He went over the contract from Carlson Publishing first. He said that it was their standard contract with nothing out of the ordinary. He did say that he was surprised at the amounts to purchase the right to publish and then at the amount of royalties quoted. He thought that they think the book will do very well and wanted me to do the same so I would not try to break the contract and go elsewhere. Wow! That was great news and unexpected. He said to go ahead and sign the contract.

As to Becky's contract, George said that it was a standard contract for a literary agent, and the percentages of royalties was not out of line for the industry. He said to go ahead and sign this one too.

This is a monumental day for me! The contracts have been signed and are sent! I CAN RESIGN!!!!!!!

I have to email Sara! I think she will be surprised and thrilled for me. I can't wait to hear back from her.

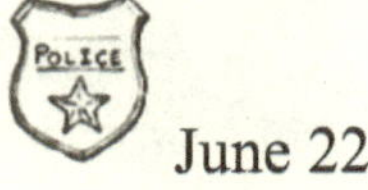

June 22

Sara called first thing this morning. At first, I thought there was a real problem, being she was calling so early. She said that everything was fine, but she needed my home address. I asked why? She said that I would find out. Once I gave it to her, she said "bye" and hung up. What the hell? No congrats? Nothing! Maybe she did not read my email yesterday. I can't believe she would not say something about my news. She is the one who put me on this path.

I'll check my email when I get home tonight and see what her reaction is. Time to go back into HELL.

Holy Crap!!! When I got home, I had one of the largest gift baskets I have ever seen at my door. The thing had to weigh two or three pounds. There were two bottles of champagne, cheeses, meats, crackers, munchies…you name it. It was from Sara with a card of congratulations. And not sure if she realized it was signed "Love Sara"! A general love, just a fleeting moment in the congratulation's moment? I don't know. I'm trying not to read too much into it. I need to give her a call and give her a great big THANK YOU!

I gave Sara a call. She picked up, I think on the first ring. I thanked her for the gift basket and described how surprised I was by it. She was thrilled that I liked it. I told her that I would not have to go grocery shopping for a few days as there was so much in the basket. That made her laugh. She asked how the writing was going and I told her great. I also told her that I think I made the decision not to only take a leave of absence, but to resign and write full time. She was surprised by that and asked if, I was sure. I said that I was sure. She asked what date I had in mind to be my last day. I told her that I would be submitting my letter of resignation tomorrow and that my last day would be July 10th. I also mentioned that I would be checking with our HR department before I let my boss know. There is a possibility of not just leaving but taking an early retirement, not necessarily taking the pension right away, but it would be there for the future.

I mentioned that the only problem would be when I finish the third book. What would I write about then? She chuckled a little and said that maybe we could go on some other adventures together. Damn, I think I love this woman. After what she went through in Alaska finding her sister, the fiasco in Washington State and she is still game! She said that we would talk more when she visits and maybe we could come up with something in the future, make a plan.

She said that she had to go but would be talking to me soon and would email the date she plans on arriving in Alaska along with where she will be staying. I thanked her again for the basket.

Tomorrow will be an exciting, but hard day. I wonder what HR will say. I'm sure that they will keep my inquiry about the resignation/early retirement quiet, like before. They do not want to be part of what is to be an explosion by the chief.

June 23

Marybeth in HR was surprised to see me. I told her that I needed some info and that I had some info for her. She took me into her office and asked "what's up?" I asked about my pension, was I fully vested with fifteen years of service. She was a little surprised by this question but said yes, I was, but that I was way too young to take it. I then asked if I left the force the pension would be there waiting for me when I was older, right? Again, she said yes. Marybeth has always been a very straight forward person and wanted to know why the hell I was asking these questions. Was I going somewhere, leaving the force? I sat back in my chair and told her that yes, I was leaving the force and that I planned on giving the chief my two weeks' notice today.

She just sat there, not saying anything. I asked if she was ok. No answer. I started to get worried when she suddenly said the chief is going to f'n kill you! What the hell? Why? Where are you going? Are you leaving Alaska and if not, it might be a good idea! HOLY CRAP, HOLY CRAP!!!!!!

After she settled down, I told her that no, I am not leaving Alaska or Anchorage. I explained, without any detail, that I had an opportunity to get out of police work and that I was going to give it a try. I told her that I had had enough and wanted to get out before I became any more jaded than I already was.

She finally said that she was happy for me because she had seen too many of us lose ourselves in the job and the effects it had on them personally and their families. She did have one question for me…She wanted to know if she could be there when I told the chief. She said if anything she could be a witness, just in case. I told her that I did not think that would be a good thing, that I'm sure she would get a blow by blow from the grapevine. She said that I was no fun. Before I left, I gave her a copy of my resignation letter as I'm sure the chief will destroy the one, I have for him. She wished me luck.

Telling the chief was nothing like I expected. I fully expected him to go off and blow a gasket. This was much more scary! For a few minutes after I explained that I had an opportunity out of police work and would be leaving, he said nothing, just looked at the letter and then me. No yelling or swearing. I just sat there waiting for the explosion, that never happened. Then he really surprised me. He said that since coming back from my trip last year, he had seen a subtle change. He said that he knew somehow that this was coming and that he was happy for me! I told him that I would keep doing the job to the best of my ability up to my last day on July10th.

He then said that I needed to tell Frank and wished me luck with that.

Now I have to tell Frank. It looks like lunch will be on me again.

Over lunch I told Frank that I was leaving the force. He was surprised. Unlike with Marybeth and especially the chief, I told Frank everything. Well almost. Not the part about Sara and saving her sister and her friend Jim from a vortex. I just told him that I was a published author but not under my name and that I would now be writing under my name and that I had just gotten a contract for three books. I did ask him to keep this between us. Frank said he would but had a question for me. Ok? When I become rich and famous would I still have lunch with him, and would he get free author signed books? I said yes to both.

Frank finally asked when my last day would be. I told him July 10th. Frank was really surprised by the date. He said that is only about two weeks from now. Then he wanted the scoop on what the Chief said. Unfortunately, we got a call and had to put the rest of the conversation on hold. We had to get back to the ugly real world.

I know, I keep writing the same thing about my job but thankfully it will change in only less than two weeks! Not planning on writing tonight. The usual relax, dinner, a drink and bed.

June 24

Boy does news move fast! I think just about everyone knows that I am leaving. I hardly got in the door when I had several people come up to me and ask if it's true. They have also asked if I'll be spending the rest of my time on desk duty. I told them no. I will be going about my day(s) as usual dealing with the dreadful side of Anchorage. I should have just put a sign on my back saying YES, ITS TRUE! I think they all meant well it just got old real fast.

Thankfully, the day was uneventful. Just some minor disputes and one robbery to work on. Tomorrow is another day but one more closer to my new beginning.

June 25

SARA

June 24

Parker and I have been emailing and talking. Parker is so excited about the books. He came up with a great idea for three books, the first based on his dealings with my sister Marni and her journey to find her friend Jim. Then using my trip, to find my sister and then our trip to Washington State. He emailed me that his agent and publisher are on board. After reading the pages he sent, I think the book will be really good. A thought just hit me. How did he get an agent so quickly and the agent able to get the book deal pulled together so fast? I thought getting an agent was not an easy thing and then the publisher too. Am I missing something, or does he just have good contacts or just people he knows? I'm curious. I will need to ask when I see him in roughly two weeks.

I think we are back to our old selves after our Washington trip. I had no idea how mad I could get until then. I think that I started to really care about him and that is why I got so mad. I have to be careful; I really like this guy.

I need to call my travel agent Amy and get my Alaska trip planned out and booked. I plan on staying at the same hotel in Anchorage, the Historic Anchorage Hotel. Initially I'm thinking two weeks. Hopefully, I don't get the haunted room like before as I can see them now, courtesy of the vortex, and I really do not want to deal with whatever or whoever is there.

Ok, enough…time to call Amy.

June 25

Not much to write about today. Amy got back to me with details for my July trip to see Parker. I asked if I was going to have the same room as last time. She was not sure but could check with the hotel and find out. I asked her to look into it as I did not want to stay in that room again. I told her to just make sure it was either a suite or junior suite. Amy asked why? I told her that the room was haunted. She said what? Really? So, I told her about my research into the hotel and my experience in the room. She said ok, but I don't think she believed me.

I plan on getting ready for this trip over the next couple of weeks. No rushing this time. I think I'll make a day-by-day list, so I am not overwhelmed.

June 26

God! What an awful night. Something or someone kept waking me up. I also have a feeling that something horrible is about to happen or will happen. I just can't shake the feeling. It's also like someone or something is reaching out to me but can't quite make contact. I know that I can see ghosts. In Washington I was able to help a little boy and his dog find his parents who were waiting for him on the other side. That was such a great feeling helping them and sort of knowing that there is something out there when we die.

I'm going to reach out to Marni and make sure she is ok and if she is then maybe the feeling will go away.

I finally got a hold of Marni this evening and she is fine. She also mentioned that any of our shared friends/acquaintances are ok too. She has not had any phone calls with bad news and if she did, she would call right away. I then asked her the question that I know I shouldn't. "Have you had any dreams about anyone?" I think she realized how freaked I was/am in order to bring this up and did not go off on me. She said no, no dreams but she would let me know if she did. She also said that the only reason why she had the dreams of Jim was to find him. He reached out to her. As far as she was concerned it was a one-time thing.

Ok, then what is this? It has been on my mind all day and the feeling seems to be getting stronger, more intense.

Ok, I need to distract myself. A strong drink and dinner in front of the tv with a good movie. Keep busy.

Ok, WHAT THE HELL!!! I was heading into the kitchen to put my plate in the dishwasher, and I swear that for an instant I saw Parker. Like he was here but not. Oh my god, is he in trouble? I did not think of him earlier. I told myself not to panic, but I did. I called Parker's cell and land line and got no answer. I also sent him an email. I have to tell myself that his not answering could be for a very normal reason. Out with friends, working late and could not answer his cell, on a date. Then my mind went to a car accident, a fall, getting hurt on the job! Oh, crap. He's a cop and I know he sometimes deals with really bad people.

Ok, don't panic. It's late and there is not much I can do tonight. I can try to call Mike tomorrow if I don't hear from Parker by noon. Or I could call the Anchorage police station and see if they have any info, they will give me.

It is going to be a long night.

June 27

It is about one thirty in the morning. I had to write this down while it was still clear in my brain. I woke up with a start. Not sure why. When I looked around, I saw Parker. He was standing by the side of my bed. He was there for only a second or two. Did I just see his ghost? Is he dead? God, please no.

Morning will not come fast enough. I'm not going to wait till noon. I think I have my answer. I'm going to have a lot to do. I don't think I can sleep any more today. I'm going to pack a suitcase, call Amy first thing and tell her to get me on the next plane to Anchorage and to book the hotel, any hotel, and a rental car.

God, please don't let him be dead.

Ok, called Amy at nine a.m. and explained that I needed to get to Anchorage ASAP and to cancel all the previous arrangements but make the new arrangement for two weeks, maybe longer. She was curious and I just told her that a friend was in trouble and needed my help. She said that she would get to work on it and call me as soon as she had arrangements made. I told her any flight for late this afternoon or in the evening.

I checked my email and nothing from Parker. I looked up the number for the Anchorage police department and gave them a call. I explained that I was a friend of Detective Parker and that he was going to call me last night but did not. I told them that this was a scheduled call and he never missed them and that I was very concerned. They basically said that they could not release any info but could get a message to him. I asked if they could do a wellness check and she laughed at me and said she would put a message to call me in his in box. Well, that was a waste of time.

I called and left a message for Mike. I explained a little and that I thought Parker was in trouble. I asked him to call me if he heard anything.

I need to go into overdrive. I have already packed now I need to do some running around. Hopefully, Amy calls soon with travel info for me and hopefully Mike calls with good news.

Amy called. The soonest she could get me a flight was for today at six thirty. She also said that she has booked me at the same hotel but was not sure what room I may get. I told her no problem regarding the room, I'll deal with it. She also said that a rental car has been arranged and will be waiting for me at the airport. I thanked her and said that I had to go.

I have already arranged for a taxi to the airport. I should be in Alaska by nine thirty my time and three thirty their time. That will give me time to get to the hotel and make calls and possibly go to the police station. Hopefully with a real person there they will give me some info.

The only thing I keep saying to myself is that Parker has not appeared again. Hopefully, he is ok. I have to keep thinking that.

I'm in my room, thankfully not the haunted one from two years ago. I checked and have no messages or emails other than the normal ones. I got in later than I thought. My flight was delayed and there was a mix-up with the rental car. I need to try and relax, no news is good news, right? I've ordered some dinner to my room and once I get that I'll sit, munch, and start making phone calls.

June 28

Mike called me last night about six. He apologized for not calling sooner but he was at work, in the wilderness and did not have access to his cell phone. He said that Parker and his partner had gone to a domestic call, and both had been shot. Mike said it was all over the news. Parker was shot multiple times and it's reported that he is in critical condition. His partner Frank was shot twice and would be ok. Both are in Providence Alaska Medical Center.

After Mike's call I immediately left for the hospital. When I got there and asked to see Ben Parker, I was asked if I was family. I said no, just a good friend from Chicago and that we had planned to get together this week. Yah, ok I lied, just by two weeks. I told the person that a mutual friend had informed me what had happened and where he was. The receptionist said she would check to see if visitors were allowed.

I had no idea what to expect. When I got out of the elevator, I was surprised by the police presence. I walked toward Parker's room and was stopped by an officer. His name tag said he was Officer Beckman. He asked who I was, I introduced myself and gave him the same answer I gave the receptionist. I asked him how Parker was doing. He said not well that he had coded twice, and the doctors were able to bring him back. He said that Parker had been shot three times, two not life threatening but one hit him in the chest and nicked his heart and he had undergone emergency surgery. He said that it is still touch and go. Now I know why I saw him. He came to me, why? How would he know that I would be able to see him? Maybe he didn't, oh hell I don't know. I'll try and figure that out later. The officer showed me into Parker's room, and I was not prepared for what I saw.

Parker was in a private room. There were wires and tubes everywhere. He did not look good. I pulled up a chair and held his hand. I had a hard time holding it together. I finally was able to talk to him. I told him to hang on, that he could do it. I said that we had travels to go on when he was better, that we had all of Alaksa to explore together and then the world. I told him that I would stay in town for however long it took for him to get back on his feet. Then I lost it. I couldn't control the shaking and tears.

Officer Beckman must have heard me. He came in and touched my shoulder and motioned for me to leave. He escorted me out to Parker's room with his arm around my shoulders as I sobbed. He took me to a waiting room, sat me down, gave me a box of tissues and a bottle of water. He sat with me until I got myself under control.

Back under control I thanked him for his kindness. He asked how I knew Parker as I had mentioned that I was from Chicago. I told him that he helped me find my sister a couple years ago and that we had stayed in touch and even traveled together. He said oh, you were the Washington trip. He mentioned that Parker was really stoked about that trip but did not say much when he got back, just that it was a good trip but complicated.

I asked him about his partner Frank. He said that he was doing well. He had been shot twice, once in the shoulder and once in his side. The one on his side luckily did not hit anything vital. I asked if I could visit Frank too. He suggested that I wait until tomorrow as he thought I needed to get some rest and not to be impolite he said you look like hell. I smiled at that. He also wanted to know if I wanted a ride back to where I was staying. I said thanks but no, I'll be ok and take it slow. I thanked him and gave him my phone number and asked him to call me if there was any change.

I did not realize how long I was at the hospital. By the time I got back it was almost ten, I was wired but exhausted. I just fell into bed.

I did not plan on going back to the hospital today. I think that I need to step back and digest what I saw and deal with my emotions. I surprised myself when I broke down. I really do care for Parker. The good news is that I have not had a call from Officer Beckman, hopefully Parker is holding his own.

I am going to take today and try to distract myself. Rather than calling around I plan to get out and walk around, distract myself. I want to find a florist and send flowers to Frank and just do some window shopping. I know with Parker being in the ICU he cannot have any flowers, at least right now. He will get some when moved to a regular room. I just need to remember not to go overboard with the flowers. Keep it simple.

Still no news….so no news is good news. I plan on having a quiet dinner in my room and plan on turning in early. Tomorrow, I plan on being at the hospital by nine a.m.

I really need to call Marni and let her know about Parker. Now I know that the feeling I had was about

Parker. Are we somehow connected, like Marni was to Jim?

I'm definitely getting a list of things to talk to Parker about. His family or lack thereof and now this connection. Would he remember appearing to me when he coded? I think we will have some very interesting conversations to come.

June 29

I was at the hospital first thing this morning. I went to Parker's room first. He was still in ICU and there was still a police presence, but not as many officers. Officer Beckmen was there too. He came up to me and asked how I was doing. I said ok. I asked how Parker was. He said that he was now stable but still unconscious. He said that the doctors were starting to get concerned that he had not started to wake up. I asked if any family had been here as if possible and if they agreed I would like to meet them. He looked uncomfortable and said that as far as he knew Parker had no family, at least in Alaska. He said that Parker kept his personal/family life to himself.

His answer surprised me. Why had I not asked Parker about his family? I didn't even ask if he was married or had a significant other. I don't think it dawned on me to ask. We were trying to find my sister and he was just the cop who helped me. Then later we were so into the Washington trip. Now I wish I had asked as I realize that I do care about him, but how much?

I thanked Officer Beckman and went in to see Parker. He looked like he was just sleeping. I pulled up a chair and just sat there holding his hand. I talked to him, telling him that he had a lot of people concerned about him, including me. I said that I was keeping Mike and his parents up to date on his condition. I told him that he had to get better, that we had a lot of traveling to do and that he had to finish his book. I told him that I had to go but would be back tomorrow and that he needed to wake up and that I wanted to see his eyes open tomorrow. I kissed his forehead and left.

I was going to stop in and see Parker's partner, Frank, but when I went by it looked like he had family with him, and I didn't want to interrupt. I'll stop tomorrow.

June 30

I was at the hospital by ten this morning. There were just a couple of police officers in the waiting room. Officer Beckmen was not one of them. I went to Parkers room and a nurse was there. She was checking his IV. I asked how he was doing. She said that he was holding his own but that he still had not woken up. They were starting to get concerned but would give him a day or two more before the doctors started to look for a reason. They know that he did not have a head wound or bleeding in the brain as they had already checked. They thought that when he went down, he hit his head, but the scan was clear. Well, that was a bit of good news.

After she left, I pulled a chair up and took Parker's hand. Somehow, I thought that if I could get his attention. So, I just sat there holding his hand and talked about our first meeting in Anchorage. How he did not believe my sister's journal and how we actually did find her and the portal. I was just babbling about anything when I could have sworn, he held my hand a little tighter. I tried not to get too excited. It could have been wishful thinking, but it wasn't! I hit the call button for the nurse. When she came in, I told her that he squeezed my hand.

The nurse asked if I was sure, and I said yes. She put a call into his doctor, and he was there, I swore, within minutes. They asked me to leave while they examined him.

The two officers that were there approached me and asked what was going on. I told them that Parker had squeezed my hand as I was babbling to him and then summoned the nurse who then summoned the doctor. They asked me to leave so they could examine him.

We waited quietly but all of us were on pins and needles. They, the officers, did not want to let anyone know what was going on until we got info from the doctor. It seemed like forever before he came out of Parkers room. He had a smile on his face. He said that Parker was not fully conscious yet but was responding to his request to squeeze his hand. He said this was very good news and that Parker should be even better tomorrow and that they would still be keeping a close eye on him.

The officers went off to make calls and I popped back into Parkers room. I held his hand and said that I would be back tomorrow, and I expected him to at least say hi. I kissed his forehead and left.

As I was leaving Parker's floor and heading to introduce myself to Parker's partner, Frank, I noticed some strange things and people that I had not noticed before. I think I was so wrapped up with my emotions and concerns about Parker that I did not think of what I might see at the hospital. The one good thing is that I have learned how to control my emotions when seeing spirits. I can walk around and, in a way, see them but not. If you don't acknowledge them, they tend to walk by you and leave you alone unless they know you can see them. Now that I am aware of them, I have to be very careful not to interact or acknowledge them in any way. I do not want to disturb them, and I don't want them to disturb me.

I did not stay long in Frank's room, maybe fifteen minutes. Parker had mentioned me to him, so he knew who I was. He thanked me for the flowers, and I gave him an update on Parker before I left.

I was not looking forward to another night in my room, so I called Mike to see if he was in town. Mark did not pick up, so I just left a message about Parker's condition.

Dinner in the restaurant downstairs and then an early night. I want to be at the hospital by nine tomorrow.

July 2

I headed to the hospital wishing and praying that Parker would be awake and able to talk. I held my breath as I approached his room. When I looked in, Parker was sitting up in the bed. I was so thrilled that he was really on the mend. He looked up and said hi or tried to. His voice was very raspy. I think it was from being intubated. He did smile and tried to ask what I was doing here.

I pulled a chair up and said that this was the date that I should have been here. Then I said ok, I'm early and that we could talk about that later. I asked how he was doing, and he gave me a thumbs up. I said that I would not stay long but told him to let me know if there was anything I could do for him while he was in here. He said that when he could talk better, yes, I could help. Just then a couple doctors came in and asked if I could leave. I said sure and told Parker that I would be back later today. He just smiled at me and mouthed thank you.

I wandered around the downtown stores and shops. I had lunch at a small restaurant and wandered around some more till about three. I then made my way back to the hospital.

When I got back to his room, he was sitting up with a tray in front of him. He had some really ugly something in a bowl. I just looked at that and then at him. We both just started to laugh. I asked how are you doing? His voice was much better and said doing good but don't make me laugh, it hurts! We then tried to talk all at once. I stopped and let him talk. He wanted to know why I was here early. I did not want to tell him that I saw his spirit and knew something was wrong. I just told him that I just wanted to surprise him, and he accepted that. I also did mention that we, once he was strong enough and home we would have a lot to talk about. I told him that his job right now was to keep recovering.

I asked if he needed anything. He said yes. He wanted his laptop. I said ok, how would I be able to get that for him. He told me that the hospital had all his belongings from when he was brought in and that he would get his stuff which included the keys to his condo. He asked if I could get it and bring it to him. He started to look tired, and I told him to arrange that when he could and that I would be back later this afternoon and if he was able to get his stuff, I would pick up the laptop and bring it to him tomorrow.

I popped back in late afternoon and Parker gave me his keys and the address to his condo. He said that his second bedroom was an office, and I would find the laptop there. He also reminded me to also grab the laptops cord. I told him that I would pick up his laptop in the morning and drop it off. I told him to let me know if he thought of anything else he might need to give me a call.

July 3

I went to Parkers condo and picked up his laptop and cord. His place was close to downtown and had a view of the mountains. His condo was not what I expected. At the same time, I had no idea what to expect, a guy's house with miss matched stuff? His place was nice and very comfortable. The furniture fit and looked comfortable giving the place a sense of warmth. The kitchen was open to the living room with a counter separating the two and looked clean. One thing that I did do was check his frig. Luckily, there was not much in there and I didn't find anything that needed to be thrown out. I found his laptop and got out of there. I really wanted to snoop around but I would not do that to him.

One thing that I did notice was he had several books from an author by the name of Ben Parson in the bedroom he used as an office. The one I looked at was a cop story. I'm surprised being a cop that he likes to read cop stories. Maybe he reads them for fun, who knows.

I got to the hospital about eleven. Parker was sitting up and looked much better. He even sounded better too. I gave him his laptop and keys. We chatted for about an hour. I asked him how he was feeling. He said sore but better. He mentioned that they had him up walking this morning and that went pretty well but tired him out. He said that he had a lot to tell me but wanted to wait until he was out of the hospital so he would be off all the pain medication and have a clear mind. He asked how long I was planning on staying. I told him as long as he needed or wanted me to. He said that I did not have to stay, he would be ok. I told him that I had planned on being here anyway and that I would stay the two weeks we talked about. I asked if he had any idea of when they would release him? He told me that he had asked that question this morning and did not get a straight answer from his doctor. He started to chuckle and said that he should use his interrogation strategies on him.

The whole time we were talking I kept thinking that I needed to tell him about the ghost thing, full disclosure and how much I wanted to explore places and areas with unresolved mysteries, myths, hauntings…the unusual but not alone, with him. This would be good for him too, more stories for future books. With Parker on the mend, God willing, we will have time.

I left after about an hour and told Parker that I would be back tomorrow.

Mike called me this afternoon and asked how Parker was doing. I told him that he is better, awake and talking normally and that they had him up and walking. Mike said that he was in town and asked if I would like some company for dinner. I immediately said yes.

Had a great time with Mike. We were able to get caught up. It was fascinating when he described what he does as a ranger. He said no two days are the same. He got his degree and is qualified to collect environmental data on plant and wildlife habitats within the park. He said that the process and tools used are always updated and plans on taking additional course work to keep up.
I asked about his parents, and they are doing well just a little slower.

It was so nice not to have a meal by myself or in my room. I mentioned to Mike that anytime while I'm here I'd be up for dinner again and maybe with his parents too.

July 4

Before I left for the hospital I stopped at the front desk of the hotel and asked if the dining room would be open today, holiday and all. They said yes as most of the guests were from out of town. She also said that the bar will have a special menu of burgers, BBQ, and other things if I didn't want to order off the regular dinner menu in the dining room. Well, that's a relief, I won't have to dive around looking for something open and right now BBQ sounds really good. The desk clerk also mentioned that there will be fireworks about ten this evening and the park was within walking distance.

I got to the hospital about ten thirty and panicked. Parker was not in his room. I just stood there for a few minutes and just as I turned to go to the nurse's station there was Parker in the doorway with his IV pole and a nurse. He just grinned at me and said they had been out for a walk. The nurse got him back into the bed and said he would get him something to drink.

We chatted for a while and Parker said that the doctor mentioned that if he kept improving, they would most likely let him go home within a couple of days. He said that the only issue was that he lived alone. They did not want him by himself for at least a week or two and someone would need to drive him to follow up appointments until cleared to drive. He said that he was thinking of hiring home health just to get out of the hospital. I have to admit I was hurt that he would not think of me to help as I'm here. I wanted to smack him upside his head but knew I couldn't.

I just sat there and looked at him, with what I hoped, had a look of REALLY on my face. For a detective he did not seem to pick up on this.

I finally said that I could help. He said no, he could not ask that of me. I asked why not as I was planning on being here for a couple of weeks anyway. I told him that it would be no problem. My hotel is just fifteen minutes from his condo. I could be there with him during the day, get him to bed and return in the morning. I also told him that I have my rental car and could take him to any appointments. I also said that for the first couple of days I could stay at his place, that his couch looked comfortable and that I would not take no for an answer. He finally agreed. Parker gave me his keys and some personal items to bring back to his condo. He also asked me to check his mailbox that it was most likely overflowing. He said to just put it all in his office and he would go through it when he got home.

July 8

The past few days have been crazy. Where to start. My last entry was July 4. Nothing much happened for a couple of days other than visiting Parker. Parker called me on the 6th and said that he would be released on the 7th. Thank God, he called me in the morning. I asked if he knew of any dietary restrictions. He said not that he knew of, that he was able to order anything from the hospital's menu. I asked if he wanted anything special as I would hit the market. He told me that anything would be better than the hospital food.

I spent most of the morning at the grocery and special food stores trying to get a variety of items for breakfast, lunches, and dinners. I think I went a little overboard, but I had no idea what he liked or didn't like. I got about a weeks' worth of meals and then some. After putting things away, I dusted and vacuumed the place. I was going to change the sheets but thought that might be going too far. I was ready.

I was at the hospital on the 7th by nine a.m. When I got there, he was still in his room, and I realized that he had nothing to wear to get home. I'm not sure he even thought of this. I asked what I could get for him as it was only a fifteen or twenty-minute ride back to his place and he was not going to ride in my car with his naked butt. He looked at me like what!!? Then started laughing. The laughing did not last long as it caused him a lot of pain. Just then the nurse came in and asked what was so funny. Parker explained my comment and she chuckled. She said that if he did not have anything to wear, she would get him some scrubs to wear home, saving me the trip. She said that she would be back shortly with them and that the doctor should be in shortly to go over and give him a copy of his release instructions and prescriptions.

The doctor came in before the nurse got back and gave Parker about twenty-five pages of instructions along with two prescriptions. With what Parker went through I would have thought he would have multiple scripts not just two. He explained what the prescriptions were and said to call to make an appointment for about a week from now and if he had any problems to call immediately. He shook Parkers hand and was gone. The nurse came in shortly after the doctor left with the scrubs. I told Parker that I would pull the car around while he changed and would wait for him by the release entrance.

While I was sitting in the car I was thinking to myself…..what the hell am I doing? I have no idea how to take care of someone just out of a hospital and in need of care that I had no clue about. Hell, sometimes I can't even take care of myself. About that time there was Parker being wheeled to my car.

He got into the car very gingerly with the help of the orderly who brought him down. Then I was thinking how the hell am I going to get him out of the car up the stairs and into his condo? Once he was in, I asked if he wanted to stop and get the prescriptions filled or go straight to the condo. He said that right now he was ok and to stop and get them filled and that it would save me a trip. Luckily, they had a drive thru, but they would take a while to get them filled. I asked if they delivered, and they said yes. One problem solved.

Parker looked at me and seemed mortified as we were leaving. I asked what was wrong? He said that he just realized that I paid for his prescriptions. I said yes, I know and that I'm keeping track of what you will owe me when better, he could pay me back. Damn, that money thing again is rearing its ugly head.

He just said thanks and then did not say too much on the way to his condo. When we got to the condo I parked outside of the main entrance. There were five stairs to the door and I was worried about Parker getting there. To my surprise suddenly there were four men around us. At first, I started to panic until I realized that Parker knew them. They heard he was going home and thought that he may need some help. There were two police officers that Parker knew, and they brought along a couple paramedics. They got him up the stairs, almost carrying him into his condo and into his bedroom. He thanked them and I thanked them. I asked if they would like anything to drink before they left but said no they had to get back to their specific stations.

They had set Parker up in his bedroom and when I checked he looked comfortable but tired. I asked if he needed any pain meds or anything else right now and he said no. I asked when the last time was, he had any and he said just before he left. I told him that I would be out in the living room and to let me know if he needed anything and to get some rest.

In the living room I looked over his discharge instructions. They were not hard to follow, mostly for him to take it very easy and not to do anything strenuous or physically taxing. A nurse would be stopping by in a couple of days to check his wound and change the dressing. THANK YOU, THANK YOU, I did not think of that and I'm not sure I could do that! The prescriptions were delivered, and I made a timetable of when they should be taken and left both on the counter for a reminder and easy access for both of us.

I checked on Parker several times during the afternoon, he seemed to be sleeping quietly. About three thirty he poked his head out of his room and came into the living room very slowly. I got up from the couch to help him, but he waived me off. He sat on, what I think is, HIS chair. I got a glass of water, a pain pill and gave him both. I said that according to his directions from the hospital and the bottle he was a little overdue for one. He thanked me and said he could feel it. I asked if he was hungry as he missed lunch. He said yes. I said that I had planned on a small steak, baked potato and a small salad if that was ok with him. He said that anything would be better than hospital food.

I started dinner and when ready got him to the table. He seems to be walking ok just slowly. He ate maybe half his meal and went back to his room to lay down.

Later that evening I checked on him and he was out like a light. I made my bed on the couch, turned off most of the lights and grabbed my journal and boy did I have a lot for today. I do have to say that today was not as bad as I thought it would be. Parker is mobile, just slow.

Ok, it's getting late, and I need to be up early. We will see what tomorrow brings.

July 9

I had set my alarm for six. I thought I was up early, but I heard Parker moving around in his room. I did not check as I didn't want to be a helicopter, as they say. I got myself ready and by the time I got dressed he was sitting at the dining table. He even had coffee ready for me!

I asked how he was feeling and if he had found his meds and taken them. He said that he found the pills and had already taken them and was feeling ok. He said that he could not believe how weak he felt, that just walking tired him out. I told him that breakfast would help and asked what he would like. He said that he would love some sausage, scrambled eggs, and toast and with a grin asked if he could get it while it was still hot. He explained that in the hospital the food when it arrived was cold. I said no problem. While I was making breakfast Parker asked me what I was going to do today. I looked at him and said that I would be hanging out here.

During breakfast I told him to be honest with me and to let me know if I needed to back off. But I also mentioned that he had just gotten out of the hospital and whether he wanted to admit it or not he was still in a weak state, that he needed time. He surprised me by agreeing but also said that I did not need to be here 24/7, he was mobile, just slow and that his body tells him when to slow down or if it did not like how he moved and that he would listen to it. He did not want to end up back in the hospital.

I asked him if it would be ok if I just stayed around today, hey it's your first full day home. I said that tomorrow the nurse was to come and check on him and if that went well, I would head back to the hotel as I only packed an overnight bag. I said just pretend that I'm not here unless you need something. Again, he surprised me by agreeing to my suggestion. He mentioned that he was going to try and spend some time going through his mail and then emails. I must have given him a look because he said that he would not overdo it and that he would just be sitting there and that he also had some calls to make. He suggested that I get out for some fresh air and that there was a trail that goes around his complex. He said that the views are good and that there was a small lake with benches about halfway through the trail. I think he was trying to get rid of me, not sure why. NO, I know why…. he wanted to make some calls and did not want to take the chance of me overhearing and did not want to be rude. I told him that a nice walk would do me good and that after I cleaned up, I would take him up on that. I did say that I would have my phone with me if he needed me while gone.

The trail was not far from the entrance to the building. It was a surprisingly pleasant walk. There were, what I think would be plants native to the area. After about ten-fifteen minutes a lake came into view. It was a good size lake, and I was surprised by that. I thought that it would be like in the states, wait I am in a state! Ok, what do they call it here? The lower forty? Anyhow, like other condo complexes where a small lake is built for aesthetic purposes. This one I believe was already here and they built the complex around it leaving a lot of nature in place. It was refreshing.

I found a bench close to the shore, tucked under some trees. I was a great place to sit, relax and think. As I was staring off into the distance of the lake I did not hear or see the women who, to me was suddenly there. She was not old but not young either, maybe forty-five to sixty. Her dress somehow did not fit the era. I think it may have been traditional dress. It was simple but had beading around the neckline and beading on the end of a scarf, belted at the waist. But hey, with today's fashions who knows what fits these days and may have been the fashion here. She smiled at me and sat on the opposite side of the bench from me. We just sat there in silence taking in the lake. I'm not sure how long we sat there together, maybe twenty minutes. She got up, smiled at me, and started to walk away. I watched her walk down the path and she just faded away.

Ok I freaked, a little. I did not realize that she was a ghost. On the other hand, I was not paying attention to her as she approached me. I wonder if I came here tomorrow at the same time if she would come back?

I headed back to the condo. When I got there all was quiet. I looked into Parkers bedroom, and he was asleep on the bed.

Parker was quiet the rest of the afternoon and evening, turning in early. I'm hoping that I did not, somehow tick him off about something. Time will tell.

I think that I need to talk to Parker if all goes well with the nurse tomorrow. I need to get back home in the next couple of days to attend to some business and I think he needs some time to himself.

July 10

Parker surprised me by being up before me. When I came out after showering and getting dressed, he was putting coffee on. He seemed cheerier than yesterday and helped a little with breakfast. I suggested that he let me finish as it looked like he was wincing a little and he agreed. We chatted over our food, and he said that this recovery thing was getting old, he just wanted to get back to normal. What do you say to that, to a policeman who by all accounts has been very physically active. I just said it would come.

I asked when the nurse was scheduled to come. He said in about an hour. I told him that I would give him his privacy and that I would make a run to my hotel, I needed to get some things. He said thanks and to take my time. He asked if I would mind picking up some sandwiches for lunch from his favorite restaurant. He would order them, and I would just have to pick them up. He asked if I trusted him to order one for me, I said yes. He placed the order to be picked up about noon and gave me the address and that the order was under his name.

I left Parker about 10:30 and went to the hotel. I got a couple changes of clothes and made some calls. My attorney wanted to meet with me in the next couple of days. I explained that I was in Alaska and could it wait. He said no that the documents that I requested regarding a trust that I wanted to set up were ready and they could not be signed via email. I asked if the date on the documents could be changed to a week from now as I was visiting a friend that was seriously hurt and that I was helping in his recovery while he was home. I said that I could be back on the 15th, and we could meet then. He said that he would arrange a meeting for us on the 16th to go over everything and hopefully I would not be too jet lagged. He would have his assistant email me the meeting time.

I found the restaurant easily and made my way back to Parkers condo. I got there just a little after noon. Parker was sitting in the dining room with some papers spread out on the table. He looked up and said that he would move everything in a minute. I said why not eat at the island and you can leave that where it is. We ate at the kitchen island, and I asked how it went with the nurse. He said great. The wound was healing, and he could start backing off on his pain meds and should be cleared to drive in a week.

The whole time I kept thinking that something was off between us. It is like he is holding himself in check. He is not the Parker I knew. Is it just the trauma of what he went through? Have I overstayed, do too much or not enough? Am I reading too much into how he is acting? I have to remember that I am in his house and maybe he felt that he had no choice in the matter. I can be pushy sometimes and tend to take over.

After lunch was done and cleaned up, I asked Parker if I could talk to him. I asked again if he was ok and he said yes. He wanted to know why I was asking again. I took a deep breath and said that you seem different, aloof, secretive or that I somehow offended you and you don't want to say anything.

I think he was lying to me when he said that he was just tired and that he was just not used to having someone with him, here in his home 24/7. I said ok. I brought up the fact that I needed to be home by the 16th. I also said that being he was doing well with a good report from the nurse that I would go back to the hotel and if all right with him, just check in to see if he would need anything being he could not drive. It would give him some normalcy that I think he needed and craving. Parker said that he appreciated what I had done for him and that he just needed time to not only deal with being shot but also the fact that he would be retired from the force when he is finally released medically. He said that this is not the way he wanted to leave the force.

I said that I would head back to the hotel today. I asked him to check his frig and freezer when he had time and let me know if he needed anything. I could pick up what was needed and drop it off and that I would give him a call in the morning.

I got my stuff together, which was not much, gave him a hug, a kiss on his cheek and left.

July 11

I got back to the hotel late afternoon yesterday. I unpacked my case and just sort of sat in my room. I'm convinced that I did or said something to Parker that upset him and he in turn has, in a way, shut me out. I know something is bothering him and he just won't tell me. I'm not going to push him for what it is, if he wants to tell me he will or he won't and then I think what could have been is gone. This is harder than if he would have died. Death would be final, and I would not be wondering what changed. It hurts. Before he was shot, I really thought we could travel together again. I have feelings for this man, dam it. I have to let this go, if it is to be, it will. I'll need to just be me when I'm around him.

I'm thinking of making an excuse to leave before the 15th. I'm sure he has other people who can shop for him or have stuff delivered. I really don't want to stay here the way things stand. I think I'll call Amy and see if she can arrange a flight home for early on the 13th. I need to give Parker a call and see if he needs anything and if so, I'll tell him that I will be leaving a little earlier when I drop off the groceries.

Amy got back to me, and I have a 9 a.m. flight for the 13th. I called Parker and he asked if I minded picking up some groceries. I said no, that was why I called. He gave me his list and I said I would most likely drop everything off about 2:30 – 3:00. I know in a way I am being a coward. This way I don't stay for lunch or dinner. I'll stay long enough to put things away if Parker is having a hard time moving and to tell him that I need to leave a couple days early.

I dropped off the groceries and Parker still seemed subdued or was he distracted? Hell, I don't know. He took the news that I had to leave a couple of days earlier better than I expected and did not ask any questions and I did not volunteer anything. I told him that I needed to get back to the hotel, but would it be ok if I stopped by tomorrow as I have an early flight the next day. He said that he would like that and that I should come by about noon, we would have lunch and catch up. This surprised me. Maybe he will tell me what is going on with him. I, again, gave him a quick hug and kiss on the cheek and left.

I spent the rest of my afternoon wandering around the shops near my hotel and then had dinner sent up to my room. I plan on getting all my things together in the morning.

I wonder if Parker will actually talk to me.

July 12

Things around me have been unusually quiet. Other than the lady at the lake I have not noticed anything unusual. Maybe I have just been able to ignore them or just not paying attention. In a way it unnerves me, the quiet before the storm. God, I hope not. It has been nice not having to ignore them, hey they were people, and I just don't like being rude.

I'm a bit nervous about this lunch. Is Parker going to tell me to take a hike? Speaking of hikes, I totally forgot about his book deal. Is that why he's pissed at me, that I have not asked about it? Hell, he can't blame me on that one after what happened to him. The book deal never crossed my mind until now and if that is the case, he will get a talking to.

Well, I'll find out soon, time to leave for lunch.

I didn't get back to the hotel until a little after six. Where to start? I got to Parker's and shortly after I arrived food was delivered. It was probably enough Chinese food to feed an army. Paker asked if I wanted a drink, and I said I shouldn't that a soda or water would do. As we started to eat, we just chatted about people we knew. Parker brought me up to date about his partner and how he was doing. He would to be back at work in a couple of weeks. I asked about him going back and he said that he still had to talk to HR and figure that out as his retirement date has come and gone.

It was strange. It was like we were dancing around and not saying or asking what we should, though at the time I had no idea what it would be.

When we finished, I gave Parker a hand putting the leftovers away and we sat in the living room. Parker looked uneasy and asked if he could tell me something and asked me not to judge. I said sure.

He said that this has been bothering him since he woke up in the hospital and just can't get it out of his brain. He was told that he coded twice in the hospital and that even though he was unconscious he was somehow at my house, twice. Once in my bedroom and once in my kitchen. He said that it was for only seconds and then nothing until he regained consciousness. He said that he thought it happened when he coded and somehow, for some reason he remembered it. He said that he can still see those two times like minutes ago when he closes his eyes. He said that it is driving him nuts, or that he is nuts.

The whole time I'm thinking, holy crap, I need to tell him the truth about seeing ghosts. I moved closer to him and took his hand. He just looked at me like "what"? While holding his hand I told him that I had seen him in my kitchen and bedroom like he just like you told me. I explained that is why I came early.

When I saw him, I thought he had died and that he did twice for a few seconds. I said that I had no idea what happened, how or why he came to me. It may have been simply me being on his mind, our getting together to plan another trip. I told him how I just dropped everything and got here as soon as possible and that is when I was told what happened, by Mike.

He sat there in silence just holding my hand. I then said there is more. I told him that something happened to me in the vortex. He said I thought you did not remember anything, and I said that is correct, I don't. I said that a few months after I got home, I started noticing things, people, and animals that no one seemed to see or interact with. It took me a while to realize that I could see ghosts and that it really freaked me out. I told him that I did some research online and that some people who go through a traumatic experience sometimes can see or sense things they could not before. Then I learned to not notice them so I would not have to interact with them.

He let go of my hand and sat back. He just sat there saying nothing. He then looked at me and said God I wish I could have a stiff drink right now. Then he asked if I was talking to a ghost in Washington, in the yard the day I left. He said that he saw me talking to the air, nothing or no one in the yard. I told him that he was right that it was a little boy and his dog, that they, the boy, and dog, got to go home.

We continued to talk about this and any possible ramifications or as he put it how cool it was to talk to people who may have been gone for years or centuries!

He wanted to know why I did not tell him about it. I told him that I was still dealing with how this worked and how to handle it. Also, most people would most likely think I'm nuts, yeah right you see ghosts. He chuckled at that and said I was probably right.

Parker stood up unexpectedly and went to his office. When he came out, he had a few books in his hands that I had noticed when picking up his laptop. He said that it was his turn to confess. I just looked at him and he handed me the books. I told him that I had noticed them and thought it strange that a cop would want to read crime stories. He looked at me and said that he does not read them that he wrote them and used a pen name. What!!!! I told him that he just answered a question that I had. How he got an agent so fast as I had heard that it was not an easy thing to do in publishing.

He then got really serious and said he wanted to thank me, that without my sister Marni and me traipsing through Alaska then the two of us in Washington State he would not be in this position. I just grinned at him and asked when the next adventure was. He smiled back at me and said that we had time to plan, he had a book on deadline and still had some recuperating to do.

I was so happy!! The air had been cleared and we both revealed secrets that each of us thought would upset the other. I think he was surprised that I did not go off on him about being an author and I was thrilled that he believed me about the ghost thing.

It was getting late and said I had to get back to the hotel as I had an early flight in the morning. I told him that I would call and let him know when I got home and that we could start thinking about our next adventure. I suggested Alaska as it has so many mysteries and lore and once done here, we could expand to the world.

He walked me to the door and said that he wanted to ask me to stay but knew I couldn't. I told him that I would be back.

He then took me gently in his arms and kissed me, really kissed me and I think my knees went weak for a moment. He let me go, gently kissed me one more time and I left.

Marilyn Carlsson worked in the commercial lending department of banks for years and recently retired.

She has always been interested in the mysteries of the world, ancient / lost cities, haunted places, the unknown. Alaska was the perfect setting for her first foray into writing, **The Journals - Alaska,** as she spent two weeks there years ago and used her memories of the places, she visited to inspire her.

She currently lives in a suburb of Chicago with her dog Nala.

www.ingramcontent.com/pod-product-compliance
Lightning Source LLC
La Vergne TN
LVHW091101150826
845673LV00002B/667

* 9 7 9 8 9 8 8 4 7 1 5 1 6 *